P9-CDJ-476

Walking with the dead

Walking with the Dead

Walking with the Dead

L.M. Falcone

Kids Can Press

Kids Can Press acknowledges the financial support of the Government of Ontario,
through the Ontario Media Development Corporation's Ontario Book Initiative;
the Ontario Arts Council; the Canada Council for the Arts; and the Government
of Canada, through the BPIDP, for our publishing activity.

Published in Canada by
Kids Can Press Ltd.
29 Birch Avenue
Toronto, ON M4V 1E2

Published in the U.S. by
Kids Can Press Ltd.
2250 Military Road
Tonawanda, NY 14150

www.kidscanpress.com

Edited by Charis Wahl
Designed by Marie Bartholomew
Interior graphics by Sherill Chapman

Printed and bound in Canada

CM 05 0 9 8 7 6 5 4 3 2 1
CM PA 05 0 9 8 7 6 5 4 3 2 1

National Library of Canada Cataloguing in Publication Data

Falcone, L. M. (Lucy M.), (date.)
     Walking with the dead / L.M. Falcone.

ISBN 1-55337-708-7 (bound).   ISBN 1-55337-709-5 (pbk.)
I. Title.

PS8561.A574W34 2005   jC813'.6   C2004-903283-6

Kids Can Press is a *corus*™ Entertainment company

TO Jay Ettinger,
MY companion on the path

TO Adrian Zita Bennett —
thanks for the great title!

TO the divine spirit that moves in me
in such wondrous ways

1

When you're one of the smaller kids in class and lifting anything bigger than a bagel is an effort, guys like Slug come after you. Actually, Slug comes after a lot of kids, but it's my neck I'm worried about. He's been forcing me to pay life insurance — five bucks a week or he'll beat the crap out of me. We're into our seventh month, and coming up with the money is stressing me out big time.

I started by going through my savings, but they ran out pretty quick, so now I do odd jobs. It hasn't been easy. Mrs. Cleary, down the block, once gave me a whole two bucks for washing *and* polishing her car. I couldn't believe it. My arms ached so much I walked like a gorilla for a week. So far, I've managed to pay on time. But after each payment, I barely have enough money left for a doughnut … a day-old doughnut.

Uh-oh! Here he comes. Excuse me while I jump into this rosebush.

"OWWWW!"

Usually I just hand over the five bucks and

thank Slug for not hurting me. But this week I'm short by fifty cents. Why don't I just hand over the $4.50 and promise to cough up the rest tomorrow? Simple. When you're short, even by a nickel, Slug slugs you. Hard. And if you completely miss a payment — you're dead meat.

There've been lots of times I've wanted to tell my dad what was going on, but he has enough problems. Since Mom died — three years ago — he hasn't been able to concentrate on business. We live over a shop that belonged to my grandfather. It was once a funeral parlor, but Grandpa said there were way too many spooky sounds during the night, so he turned it into a kind of weird museum called Oddities. It displays "unusual" items — shrunken heads, petrified hands, mannequins made completely out of marshmallows. Sort of a Ripley's Believe It or Not, only not as interesting.

It hadn't been doing very well for a long time, so finally Dad just closed it down. Since then he's been sitting around the house watching TV. But last week he heard about this airport auction where they sell off all kinds of things that people forget when they get off the plane — leather jackets, computers, skis, you name it. How could anybody forget their skis? Wouldn't you notice when you were swooshing down some mountain?

Anyway, I was hoping Dad would come home with something I'd like. Maybe some videos or a suitcase full of money. Instead, he showed up with a big wooden crate that he put in the basement under the museum. So what was in the crate? A coffin. You heard me right — a *coffin*. And inside the coffin was an ancient Greek corpse. I'm not kidding. Dad said it must have been part of a traveling exhibit and somehow got left behind. Why nobody claimed it doesn't make sense. But, hey, sitting in a thorny rosebush didn't make sense either, but here I was, with sharp thorns about to dig into my eyeballs, on the last Saturday of summer holidays.

What was taking Slug so long? I knew he was a slow walker — anybody his size would be — but this was too slow even for him. With the sun beating down on my head, I knew I couldn't sit there all day, so I finally worked up the nerve to back out of the bush. I moved really carefully, but my hair must have caught on some humongous thorn because all of a sudden a chunk of it got ripped right out of my skull.

Screaming isn't something you can always control. At least I couldn't. And guess what?

Slug just *happened* to be walking by at that *exact* moment. Now, any normal person would at least ask why I was sitting in the middle of a rose-bush, but no.

"Where's my money, squirt?" is all he said.

I handed over the $4.50, got punched and went home.

2

I started this school year the same way I started every year, with one goal — to get Rosalie DiNardo to like me. She's the smartest and, to me anyway, the prettiest girl in the class. I was getting nowhere, as usual, so by October I decided to volunteer at the same place she does, a seniors' home called Forest View.

"Just make yourself a name tag," the lady at the desk said.

My first job was to push an old man named Mr. Lucas around the grounds in his wheelchair. It was a nice day and he was kind of funny and easy to talk to. Next I pushed Mr. Khan, then Mr. Morris and finally Mrs. Lee, who was the size of a hippo. I kept looking around for Rosalie, hoping she'd see me and think I was some kind of hero or something. She was nowhere in sight.

With the corpse in the basement, Dad's mind got to working overtime. He came up with the bright idea of renovating the museum and having a grand reopening. It was almost Halloween, so it seemed the perfect time to do it. He talked about the new spooky exhibits he was going to add, and he figured people would pay good money to see a genuine, zillion-year-old corpse. I had to agree with him. It was all I could do not to bring my cousin Freddie over for a look, but I promised Dad I wouldn't and I never break a promise.

It takes a lot of work to renovate something as big as Oddities. Since Dad couldn't afford to hire help, I did what I could, and my Uncle Charlie, Freddie's dad, came by every night after work.

As the days passed, I started noticing a change. Dad was getting, I don't know, happier, I guess. Uncle Charlie noticed, too. Another change was that Dad started going to the library and bringing home tons of books on Greek myths and legends. He wanted to be able to talk to visitors about the corpse like an expert. Dad's favorite saying is "Knowledge is power," so he studied pretty hard. Besides, he knew this was his last chance. If people didn't start coming back to Oddities, he'd have to shut down for good.

One day, I raced home from school, trying to outrun a storm. Made it just in time. The first crack of thunder hit as I was going up the stairs to our apartment. Dad was sitting at the kitchen table, his nose in a book.

"Listen to this, Alex," he said, excitement in his voice. "In ancient Greece it was believed that the souls of the newly dead went to live in the Underworld. To get there, souls were ferried across the River Styx by a boatman named Charon. But he would ferry only those souls that were buried with a gold coin in their mouth."

My eyebrows went up. This was more interesting than *The Three Stooges* reruns, which is what I usually watch when I get home. I grabbed a Pop-Tart and pulled up a chair.

"The gold coin was payment for safe passage. Without it, Charon would refuse his services and the dead would remain stranded on the banks of the river ... forever denied their eternal rest. They became known as 'the lost souls.'"

Dad took off his glasses and I saw a light in his eyes that I hadn't seen in a long time. "I think we've got a winner here, son." He smiled at me. I handed him half my Pop-Tart.

As we sat there, a thought hit me. "Dad? If what the book says is true, there should be a gold coin in the corpse's mouth."

"There should be. I doubt a soul could take

the actual coin itself, but you never know."

He slipped on his glasses and flipped back a few pages. "It says here … 'On rare occasions, enemies would not allow family members to put the gold coin in the corpse's mouth, as punishment for something the dead person had done.'" Dad leaned back on his chair. "I'd hate to think our corpse's soul was still stranded at the river."

"Can we check?"

Dad put the book down. "Let's go."

We went downstairs into Oddities. White canvas sheets covered almost everything, paint cans were all over the floor, and shelves had been taken down and stacked in the corner.

A huge flash of lightning lit up the room. The clap of thunder that followed was so loud the room shook and some plaster fell. Dad pulled me back just as it crashed to the floor.

"That was close," he said. "Be careful."

We made our way to the basement door. Dad reached out and flicked on the switch, but as soon as the light came on, we heard a pop and the bulb went out. "That's odd," he said. "I put in a new bulb just last week."

The light from the back porch was bright

enough to guide our way down, but as we walked through the basement, it got dimmer and dimmer. Dad stopped and lifted a flashlight from a shelf near the furnace. The glow made the room look creepy.

When we got to the crate, Dad and I lifted the lid. Then we slowly opened the coffin and looked at our corpse. He seemed even uglier in this light, with his stretched gray skin and sunken eyes. A shiver ran down my back. Maybe it wasn't such a good idea after all.

"The ancient Greeks believed that a person's soul left the body through the mouth," said Dad. "So it was always left open."

"That way it could grab the coin on its way out, right?"

Dad smiled, leaned over and shone the light on the corpse's face. "The mouth isn't open," he said, sounding disappointed. Then he looked up at me. "Poor thing must have had enemies."

I felt sorry for our corpse. Here he was, ready to help Dad's business, and all these centuries his soul's been waiting by the river. "Can't we do something?"

"Like what?"

"Like buy a gold coin and put it in his mouth … or *on* his mouth."

"I think it's a little late for that, son."

"What if he's still standing there on the shore while every other soul goes across!"

Dad looked surprised at my outburst. "Alex. That's just a legend."

"What if it *isn't*? Do you want to take that chance?" Dad didn't answer. "There's got to be a gold coin *somewhere*."

"Of course, at a coin shop. But I doubt we'd get one for less than a hundred dollars."

"You're kidding? For one measly coin?"

Dad nodded. "At the very least — some cost *thousands*."

No way could we afford a hundred dollars. Everything Dad had was going into the renovations, and I still owed Slug his protection money.

3

The next day after school, as I walked through the park to Forest View, all I could think about was the corpse's soul waiting all alone.

I was still thinking about him when I ran into Rosalie on the second floor. She was surprised to see me. "Alex? You're volunteering here?"

"Sure," I responded. "I love old people."

That's when Rosalie did something I never, in my wildest dreams, ever expected. She reached out and stroked my cheek. Not having a mom and all, I don't get my cheek stroked much. I practically started bawling. "Gotta go," I mumbled. "Mr. Lucas needs his dentures brushed."

I didn't know if Mr. Lucas even wore dentures, but I had to get away — fast.

Mr. Lucas was in the bathroom when I got to his room, so I sat on the bed and waited. I noticed a photo album on his night table, slid it onto the pillow and flipped through it.

When I went to put the album back, I spotted the corner of something sticking out from under the bed. I pulled it out.

Page after page had different coins tucked into little clear plastic pockets, and each pocket had a label on it. My hands started to shake. Maybe, just maybe ... About halfway through I found it — a gold coin! The label said "British Sovereign — Edward VII." So that's what one looks like.

Just then the bathroom door opened and Mr. Lucas rolled out in his wheelchair. I asked him about his coin collection. He said he'd started it when he was a teenager, and it was the only thing he brought with him when he came to Forest View. That and the photo album.

I told Mr. Lucas about the corpse my dad had bought and how he was going to display it at the reopening of Oddities. And about the legend that says souls without a gold coin couldn't get across the river to the Underworld. "Our corpse doesn't have one," I said. Then, without my even asking, Mr. Lucas slowly pulled the British Sovereign out of its pocket and handed it to me.

"I — I couldn't take it, sir," I stammered.

"Nonsense," he said. "It isn't doing anybody any good sitting here."

It just didn't seem right. "No. No. Thank you. It's probably too late anyway. He's been dead a zillion years."

Mr. Lucas looked at me with gentle eyes. "Then he's waited long enough, don't you think?"

4

When I got home, I headed straight to the basement. Flicking on the flashlight Dad had left on the top step, I went down the rickety stairs. I made my way over to the crate, set the flashlight on a shelf, aiming the beam at the coffin, then used both hands to lift the lid. This time, the corpse didn't seem as ugly. I leaned over his body and said, "This is your lucky day." Reaching into my back pocket, I pulled out the gold coin and held it up in front of his face. "Look what I've got."

I gently placed the coin on the corpse's mouth. The gold shone in the light.

"I hope it's not too late."

Back upstairs I made myself three peanut butter sandwiches, poured a glass of juice and went to my room. As I neared the door I got a funny feeling, sort of like when you're seasick on a boat. The design on the rug suddenly went blurry and I had to press my hand against the wall to keep my balance. I blinked a couple of times and shook my head. Then, just like that, everything went back to normal.

I knew I should do my homework but I started reading one of Dad's library books instead. It was all about gorgons and someone named Medusa. I must've fallen asleep because the next thing I knew, a sound woke me. Whenever Dad couldn't sleep, he'd head to the kitchen and put on a pot of coffee. He'd been doing this a lot since Mom died.

There it was again — the same sound, only louder.

I slipped off the bed and swung open the door. Whoa! I gasped and pulled myself back. The hallway had disappeared *completely*! I was looking out over the night sky.

I edged closer to the door frame and looked down. Far below I saw a large boat floating in a thick mist. At the front of the boat, rowing with a long pole, was someone wearing a dark cloak with a hood.

5

The next morning I lay on the floor for a long time. Yes, I'd fallen out of bed, but I hadn't felt a thing. As I lay there thinking, I couldn't shake the feeling, deep down, that the dream — and the boat — were real.

After school I told Freddie what happened. He laughed and said he had crazy dreams, too, especially after eating anchovy pizza. I didn't blame him for not believing me — I wasn't sure I believed me either.

I walked Freddie to the bus stop — he had a dentist appointment downtown. Along the way we spotted a whole line of flyers that Dad and Uncle Charlie had posted along a fence. "They look pretty good," said Freddie, jogging over to take a closer look.

The flyer showed the front of Oddities, with pictures of mummies and werewolves and witches along the sides. It announced the grand reopening and also the Haunted Walking Tour that was starting tomorrow night. Dad figured the tour would get people in the mood for

Halloween and then, if they liked it and told their friends, by the time Oddities reopened, lots of customers would come.

"I sure hope people show up," I said.

"They will. Don't worry so much."

Near the bus stop we noticed dark clouds in the distance. "What's *with* this weather?" Freddie asked.

Just then the bus came around the corner and he took off. "Good luck with Rosalie!" he shouted over his shoulder.

As I crossed the park, it started getting really dark. Black clouds rolled across the sky and, suddenly, a streak of lightning flashed. I remembered something from science class — lightning strikes the highest point, so don't take shelter under trees. That was easy. There were no trees. Just grass. I started walking faster. Two more flashes zigzagged just ahead. The hair on the back of my neck stood up.

Then everything went really quiet.

I glanced around. The leaves had stopped moving. The birds had stopped singing. Not one person was in sight.

Something strange was going on.

That's when I realized *I* was the tallest point. I took off at full speed for the other side of the park. The air around me got even darker, and then I saw a streak of bright, white light. My head snapped back and my body lifted right off the ground. The next thing I knew, I was flying backward through the air and landed, hard. All the breath had been knocked out of me, and there was an awful smell of something burning. What was it? I tried to get up but couldn't move.

So I just lay there, staring at the sky.

After a while, everything got light again. Some feeling came back into my body and I managed to get up on my hands and knees. My head hurt and my legs felt shaky, but I forced myself to stand.

I should probably have gone to the hospital to get checked out, but I didn't want to wait for hours in emergency and I really did feel okay, sort of.

When I got to Forest View, I ran into Rosalie. She was feeding Mrs. Pirri and asked if I'd heard about poor Mr. Lucas.

I shook my head.

"He went crazy."

"*What*?"

She nodded. "He's been shouting at everybody,

calling them thieves. Even broke into people's rooms and pulled everything out of their drawers. It took three orderlies to restrain him."

I thought I was going to throw up. I knew why Mr. Lucas had gone crazy. His gold coin was gone and he'd forgotten he'd lent it to me. It was all my fault.

I raced to the second floor. When I got to Mr. Lucas's room, I was shocked to find him lying on his bed with his wrists strapped to the side bars. He was staring at the ceiling. "Mr. Lucas?" I said softly. "It's Alex."

He didn't look at me.

Pulling a chair closer, I sat down. "Mr. Lucas, I don't know if you can hear me, but I just want to say I'm sorry. I'm the one who took your coin. Don't you remember?" Mr. Lucas continued to stare at the ceiling. His eyes never blinked. "It was for the Greek corpse. You said to give it to him. Please remember." There was no response. I felt awful.

Just then Mr. Lucas's eyes blinked. I jumped up. "Mr. Lucas! Can you hear me? It's Alex!"

He slowly turned his head. I thought he was coming out of it. When he looked at me I smiled. But he didn't smile back — just screamed, "Thief! Thief!"

"No! Mr. Lucas! You gave me the coin!"

Mr. Lucas's face turned red and he yanked at the straps. "Thief!!"

It was no use trying to explain. Not when he was like this.

I raced out of the room.

6

I was going to tell Dad what had happened, but he was on the phone, practically begging for a newspaper article to be written about the reopening of Oddities. "Yes, I am taking out an ad, but it's something your readers might be interested in, what with Halloween just around the corner. Local history, right?" I guess it didn't work because Dad's voice got really low. "Thank you anyway."

Dad didn't say anything for a long time, then mumbled, "We really need some publicity before the reopening to boost ticket sales."

"The flyers look great," I said, trying to cheer him up. "They'll bring people in."

We heard footsteps on the stairs, and then Freddie and Uncle Charlie walked in carrying a big wooden sign and grinning. "Hey! Take a look at this!" said Uncle Charlie.

BEWARE! IT'S COMING ...

ODDITIES

GRAND REOPENING
SATURDAY, OCTOBER 15
DOORS OPEN AT MIDNIGHT
(ARE YOU AFRAID OF THE DARK?)

"Where'd you get that?" asked Dad.

"My bowling buddy, Nick, works part-time at a print shop. You don't have to pay till next month."

Dad was so happy to hear some good news I didn't have the heart to tell him about Mr. Lucas or being hit by lightning.

We all headed down to Oddities. I opened the door, but when my hand touched the handle, I got a huge shock. "Ouch!!"

Uncle Charlie heard the zapping sound. "You okay, Alex? That was a doozie!"

"Yeah, I'm okay." Actually, I wasn't. The shock had gone up my arm and into my brain. My head really hurt.

The museum looked great. There were special lights, and Dad had set up a sound system to pipe in scary music. All the exhibits had been cleaned and there were lots of new ones, too. My favorite was a special mirror. When you looked at yourself, you saw your face *and* your skeleton. And one whole room had been turned into a corn maze with three evil-looking scarecrows.

The four of us worked together putting special orange lights in the Goraporium. It was a chamber of gory things, like a bloody guillotine with severed heads in a bucket, pretend rats eating a corpse, and skulls with worms crawling out of them. They weren't real worms, but they sure moved like they were.

While we worked, Dad told us the places he was going to take people during the Haunted Walking Tour the next night — the old mill, the covered bridge and the alleys behind Darcy Street. Every spot had some mysterious haunting because of deaths that had happened there. Then he told us a couple of stories he was going to use and asked for suggestions on how to make the tour scarier.

Uncle Charlie suggested adding gimmicks and came up with a plan. He would hide inside the old mill, and right after the part where Dad tells about the owner's son climbing up the moving wheel and getting crushed, he'd turn the wheel on.

That was a great idea!

Freddie said he'd bought a spooky sound-effects tape for a Halloween party a couple of years ago. He'd try to find it. "There's a howling wind sound that'd fit in great with the witch flying through the covered bridge."

"Wonderful, Freddie!" said Dad. He seemed really excited.

Then everybody looked at me. I was the only one who hadn't come up with an idea. I lied and said I had something that was *really* scary but I wanted to check it out first. Make sure it worked.

It was after ten when we finished, and we were all exhausted. But right after crawling under the covers, I remembered the gold coin — and Mr. Lucas screaming. I headed back downstairs.

I hated what I was about to do and tried to convince myself that it was probably too late for the gold coin to help the corpse's soul anyway. But it still didn't feel right.

Opening the basement door, I flicked on the flashlight and carefully made my way down the wooden steps. They creaked loudly under my weight.

I shivered as I crossed the cold cement floor, the flashlight casting spooky shadows everywhere. When I got to the coffin, I carefully lifted the lid. Then I shone the flashlight on the corpse's face.

The coin was still there.

"I guess it was too late after all," I said. That made me feel better about what I was doing.

I gently lifted the coin and apologized for taking it back. I wished, more than anything, that he could have used it. But there was nothing I could do.

The next morning, I headed straight over to Forest View, taking the shortcut past Mario's Pizza. My bad luck — Slug was standing right there, with Zack and Kenny, waiting. Then it hit me — he was waiting for me. And my five dollars!

"You're late, squirt."

"I'm sorry, Slug. I don't have the money this week. But I —"

Before I knew it, I was hanging upside down. Zack held one ankle, Kenny the other. They carried me up the steps and lowered me over the side of the railing. If they dropped me, my head would smash like a pumpkin.

"Hand it over, squirt."

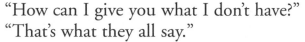

"How can I give you what I don't have?"

"That's what they all say."

"It's the truth! I haven't made a dime all week!"

"Not my problem."

As I hung there, blood rushing to my head, two guys from school came out the door. I thought they'd help. But no. They took one look and kept on moving, fast. I couldn't blame them.

"Come up with anything yet, squirt?"

"Just breakfast."

"Keep thinkin'." Slug sat on the steps.

"You can dangle me here all day but it's not going to get you your money."

"It feels good. What can I say?" Then he chuckled. "Well, look who's comin'. If it isn't your *girlfriend*, Rosalie DiNardo."

I grabbed on to a rail and twisted around. Rosalie was about two blocks away, heading *straight* for us! I couldn't let her see me like this. I'd die of embarrassment. I'd never be able to look at her again. I'd have to change my name. Move to another town. *Think ... think!* There had to be a way out.

That's when I remembered — the gold coin!

"Slug!" I shouted. "I've got something worth a whole lot more than five bucks. I'll let you keep it until I get you your money."

"Hmm ..."

Slug got up real slow.

"My back pocket."

Slug reached in, pulled out the coin.

"It's real gold," I said. "Worth at least a hundred dollars."

A huge smile crossed Slug's fat face. "I'll take the coin, squirt. But it'll cost you double to get it back. Ten bucks."

With that, he slipped the gold coin into his jean jacket pocket and headed into Mario's. Zack and Kenny pulled me up. I bolted down the steps and raced around the side of Mario's just as Rosalie got to the corner. I don't think she saw what'd happened. At least I hoped not.

I slid down the wall and sat with my head in my hands. How could I have done that? How could I just give Mr. Lucas's coin away?

I hated myself.

7

"Freddie, I need ten dollars."

Freddie was lying on the couch watching Saturday morning cartoons. "What for?"

I told him I'd borrowed a gold coin from old Mr. Lucas for one of the exhibits at Oddities. I explained how he'd gone crazy. Then I told him what Slug did. "Now he wants ten dollars or he won't give the coin back."

Freddie searched his pockets and came up with eighty-three cents.

"Is that all you've *got*?!" I was desperate.

"I had more but I bought two chocolate bars yesterday after the dentist." His eyebrows went up. "Wait a minute!"

Freddie raced down to his room. I followed close behind and saw him grab a ceramic pig off the dresser. "There's a lot more than ten bucks in here."

"That's great! Open him up!"

Freddie's face fell. "The only way to get the money is to *break* him."

"Oh." I slumped down on the bed. "Now what am I going to do?"

Freddie looked at me for a second, wrapped the pig in a towel and whacked it against the floor.

When we got to Mario's, Freddie spotted Slug and his friends. "They're at the back table," he said. "Good luck."

Taking a deep breath, I pulled open the door and marched over to Slug's table. "Well, look what the cat dragged in," said Slug, with a grin on his face. "We'd ask you to sit down, but we don't eat with squirts."

"I came to give you the ten dollars and get my gold coin back."

"And what gold coin would that be?"

What was he trying to pull?

"The one in your *jacket*, Slug." I put the money on the table in front of him. "Ten dollars."

Slug slowly reached for a french fry and bit into it. "I've changed my mind."

"We made a deal! Ten bucks and you'd give me the coin back!"

"Possession is nine-tenths of the law. And *I* have possession of the coin."

"But you said —"

"I said, I've changed my mind. Now get outta here."

"No way!"

Slug nodded toward Kenny. Kenny stood up and faced me but I pretended I didn't see him and kept looking at Slug.

"We had a deal." I made my voice sound hard.

"You're starting to bug me, squirt."

"That coin doesn't belong to you!" The people sitting nearby looked at us. I didn't care. I was so angry I could feel my blood boiling.

"Tell ya what I'm gonna do," said Slug. He leaned back and cracked his knuckles. First one hand, then the other. "You said the coin was worth a hundred bucks, right? ... Well," he slid the coins off the table into his hand, "come up with the other ninety, I'll give it back ... And that's a promise."

I felt like smashing his face with my fist. But I knew Kenny would do the same to me and I still wouldn't get the coin.

"Now, get lost, squirt. You're spoiling my appetite."

I stared at Slug's smirking face, then left. I was so mad I pushed right past Freddie and headed down the street.

"Hey, where ya goin'?"

I just kept walking.

Freddie caught up to me. "What happened?"

"Nothing."

"What d'ya mean? Did you get the coin back?"

"No."

"Why *not*? You gave him the ten bucks, didn't you?"

"Yes."

"So where's the coin?"

"In Slug's pocket!" I spit the words out.

"What's it doin' there?"

"He *changed* his *mind*! I told him the coin was worth a hundred dollars and that's what he wants before he'll give it back … Me and my big mouth."

"What're you gonna do? About Mr. Lucas, I mean."

"I don't know!" I shouted. "Just leave me alone!"

There's one thing about Freddie — even if you yell at him, he doesn't take it personally. As I walked away, he said, "So, how about lunch? I'm starving."

8

That night was the first Haunted Walking Tour. At seven thirty, Freddie came over holding a boom box and a cell phone.

"What's the phone for?"

"When I finish my sound effects at the bridge, I'm supposed to join up with the tour group and go to the old mill. Then, when your dad gets to the part in his story where the guy gets crushed, I press the Send button." Freddie slid onto a chair and reached for some leftover spaghetti. "Dad's already set it to dial a cell phone inside the mill. That way he'll know exactly when to turn on the wheel."

"Uncle Charlie thinks of everything."

After Freddie finished eating, we decided to make sure the boom box worked. He slid in his sound-effects tape and I reached out to press Play. I got another huge shock.

"Wow!" Freddie looked really surprised. "You okay?"

I shook my hand. "Yeah, I guess so."

"Maybe something's wrong with the tape recorder."

"No. It's just me," I said. "You press it."

Freddie lightly tapped the button. Nothing happened, so he pushed it all the way down. The sound of evil laughter *blasted* through the kitchen. We practically had heart attacks. He quickly turned down the volume.

"They'll love it, Freddie."

He turned the volume back up and we heard creaking doors, spooky organ music and then the sound of wind howling. "That's it," said Freddie. "That's the sound."

You'd think we were in the middle of a storm right there in the kitchen. It was that good.

I looked at my watch. It was almost eight thirty. "Time to go, Freddie."

He grabbed the boom box and headed for the door. "What are *you* doin' tonight, Alex?"

"It's a surprise."

"Make it a good one."

With that, he was out the door.

As I slumped down on a chair, I desperately tried to think of something I could do to help Dad's tour. Uh-oh. Freddie's cell phone was sitting on the table. I grabbed it and raced downstairs. "Freddie!" But he was gone.

I figured there was time before the tour group got to the old mill, so I tucked the phone in my pocket. Then I remembered something — whenever Dad changed displays at Oddities, he stored the leftover stuff in boxes in the basement. There just might be something I could use. I headed downstairs.

As I passed the corpse, I realized I hadn't closed the lid when I took the coin. No time now. I flashed the light on the shelves behind the coffin and saw two rows of boxes. The labels on the front boxes said "Skulls," "Voodoo Dolls" and "Severed Heads!"

I spotted a stool and dragged it over. Maybe there was something interesting in the severed heads box. I lifted one corner and pulled hard, thinking it would be heavy. It wasn't. The box came flying out and knocked me off balance.

I landed right in the coffin, face-to-face with the corpse.

Screaming, I tried to scramble out, but when my hand touched one of the coffin's metal handles a huge surge of electricity shot up my arm. My whole body jerked back and I was on top of the corpse again.

I lay there stunned. It was like when I'd been zapped by the lightning. Suddenly, I felt something move. Then the corpse's arms wrapped around me!

9

I broke his grip and leaped out of the coffin. As I backed against the wall, the corpse rose and turned toward me. The next thing I knew I was bolting up the stairs.

At the top I slammed the door. There was no lock, so I grabbed an old chair and was sliding it under the knob when the door burst open. I shot out the back door.

The street was totally empty. My screaming probably brought out some neighbors, but by the time they'd gotten to their doors, I was long gone. It wasn't until I reached Curzon Lane that I finally saw a car. Running to the middle of the road, I waved my arms, yelling, "STOP! STOP!"

The old man driving slammed on his brakes. He rolled down his window, stuck his head out and yelled, "What the *hell* do you think you're doing?"

"The corpse!" I screamed. "The corpse!!"

I ran to the passenger door and yanked on the handle. It was locked. Pounding my fist against the window, I shouted, "Let me in! Let me in!"

Just then the corpse came running straight for us. The old man jammed down the gas pedal and screeched away.

I took off toward the park, trying to get away, but I could hear the corpse's footsteps and branches snapping. I couldn't look back — just kept running.

From the park I spotted the light at the front entrance of Forest View. I headed straight for it, but before I could reach the door, the corpse circled around in front of me. I screamed and ran along the side of the building to the parking lot. Jumping onto the hood of the first car I came to, I stretched, gripped the top of the fence and jumped over. I landed pretty hard and rolled down a ravine, stopping myself by grabbing on to some bushes. My shoulder hurt but I didn't care. I'd gotten away.

Jogging down the ravine, I came out at the edge of the golf course. The covered bridge was just on the other side. Freddie would be there. So would Dad and the tour group.

As I made my way over the grass, I kept hearing sounds. Each time, my heart stopped. Finally I could see the bridge in the distance. Sliding down the edge of a creek, I splashed through the water and climbed up the other side.

Then I heard another splash.

I spun around. The corpse was right behind me!

I ran full out. As I neared the bridge, I looked for my dad. Where was he? I kept glancing over my shoulder every couple of seconds. The corpse was moving *unbelievably* fast. How could something so old run like that?

Suddenly, I heard the howling wind sounds. The tour group must already be inside! "Dad!" I shouted. "Help!"

The wind was blowing hard — Freddie had turned the volume way up. No one heard me. I slid down the rocks under the bridge. Freddie grinned. "Hey, Alex. Where'd *you* come from?"

Before I could answer, the corpse slid right behind me.

I turned, screamed and tried to scramble back up, but he grabbed my legs and held tight. I lay there staring at him, terrified.

"Is this guy your big surprise?" Freddie asked over the howling sounds. "He looks *great*!"

I tried to talk but no words came out.

"The tour group will be coming out the other end any second," he said. "Start screaming again then, okay?"

The corpse didn't take his eyes off me. He slowly stretched out his arm, turned his palm up and said something strange, "Se parakalo."

The sudden sound of Dad's voice made him turn his head. When he saw all the people, he ducked under the bridge and ran off.

"Hey!" whispered Freddie. "Where ya goin'?" He shook his head and sat down beside me. "Your timing was all wrong. They didn't see a thing."

When I finally got my voice back, I told Freddie what had happened. He asked me what I'd been smoking.

"It's true! Nobody knows about the corpse except me, Dad and Uncle Charlie."

"My dad knows?"

"Yes!"

"You have a corpse and you didn't even tell me?"

"I promised I wouldn't tell anybody."

"Where do you keep him?"

"In the *basement*."

"So, tell me, if he's *dead*, what's he doing running around here?"

"He woke up!"

I scrambled out from under the bridge and started running toward the group. "Dad! Dad!"

Everybody stopped and stared.

"Alex?" Dad looked confused.

"The corpse is alive! It chased me! We've gotta get everybody away from here!"

Some guys in the group laughed.

"It's true!"

"Ooooo," one of them said, "I'm shakin'."

I glared at him. More people laughed. "This isn't a *joke*. The corpse woke up and he's after me!"

"Alex is telling the truth," said Freddie. "I saw him myself."

Dad didn't know what to say. Finally he mumbled, "Just stick close to us. You'll be okay."

"*We'll* protect you," said one of the girls. Her friends giggled.

"Shut up!" I screamed. "I'm serious!"

"Alex." Dad glared at me. Then his voice went cold. "I'll see you at home."

"But, Dad!"

He walked off.

"Dad!"

The group followed him.

I was so hurt and embarrassed I turned and ran. Freddie called out, "Hey! Wait up!"

"They don't believe me," I said through clenched teeth. "*Now* what're we gonna do?"

"Tell the police! They'll catch him!"

Why hadn't I thought of it? I yanked the cell phone out of my pocket and called 911. When the operator answered, I told her all about the

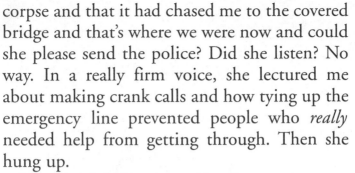

corpse and that it had chased me to the covered bridge and that's where we were now and could she please send the police? Did she listen? No way. In a really firm voice, she lectured me about making crank calls and how tying up the emergency line prevented people who *really* needed help from getting through. Then she hung up.

"She didn't believe me either!"

"Okay," said Freddie, "we go to plan B."

"What's *that*?"

"I don't know yet." Suddenly his eyes lit up. "Let's call my dad!"

"Great idea! What's his number?"

"How do I know?"

"What do you mean you don't *know*? He's *your* dad!"

"Yeah, but *that's* his phone," he said, pointing to the cell I was holding. "He borrowed the one *he's* using from somebody at work."

"Terrific. Just terrific."

"It's okay, Alex. Remember? He told me to just press Send. It's already set to dial his number!"

Freddie grabbed the phone from my hand and pressed the Send button. We put our heads together and listened.

"911."

Freddie yelled and threw the phone down. I grabbed it and punched the Off button.

"Do you think they'll know it's *us*?" Freddie cried.

Before I could answer, we heard leaves crackling. Right behind us.

10

Freddie and I didn't stop running until we got to Oddities. We bolted through the back door and slammed it. Then, gasping, we slid to the floor. Suddenly, I shot up, grabbed Freddie and pushed him back outside.

"What're you *doing*?"

"Shhhh!"

When we were safely hidden behind some bushes, I explained that I hadn't locked the door when the corpse chased me out. "He might be inside right now."

"He couldn't have gotten here before us!"

"How do *you* know? What if that wasn't him making the leaves crackle at the bridge? What if it was some squirrel or something? This is the only place he knows. Maybe he's already back — inside, waiting for us."

"And even if he *isn't* inside ... he knows where you *live*."

Our best bet was to go to Freddie's house, but when we got there, all the lights were out. "Where's your mom?"

"She didn't want Dad going to the old mill alone."

"*Nobody's* home?"

Freddie shook his head. "But don't worry. The corpse doesn't know *my* address. We're safe."

Well, we might have *been* safe, but we sure didn't feel it. After we'd made sure all the doors were locked and turned out all the lights, we sat shoulder to shoulder on the couch. It felt really creepy and we jumped at every sound.

Freddie asked, "Uh, Alex, what'd ya mean when you said the corpse woke up?"

"You know how I keep getting these shocks? Well, I got one when I was lying on top of him."

"When you were *what*?"

"I was reaching for a box behind the coffin and fell off the stool. When I tried to get up, my hand touched the metal handle and I got a huge shock. It must've gone through him, too."

"Just like Frankenstein!"

A door slammed.

"Someone's in the house!" I whispered

The door slammed again — twice. "Wait — it's okay," said Freddie. "It's just the wind banging the screen door at the front."

"Let's lock it or it'll drive us crazy."

As we made our way through the kitchen, we

decided to get weapons — just in case. Freddie grabbed a meat tenderizer and handed me a soup ladle. Raising them over our heads we tiptoed down the hall. There were narrow windows on each side of the wooden door. We peeked through to make sure the corpse wasn't standing out front, heard voices and looked farther up the street. Three doors up we saw Slug, dressed in a pirate costume, getting into the car with his parents. They drove past the house.

Freddie quietly unlocked the door while I kept a lookout through one of the windows. When the screen door blew shut again, I yelled, "Now!"

Freddie jerked open the door, locked the screen and then slammed the wooden door shut. He turned the lock.

Crash!

We froze.

The sound had come from outside. Peeking through a window, we spotted a metal garbage can rolling out onto the road. "It's not the corpse," I said. And we both relaxed.

"Garlic!" Freddie shouted. "*That's* how we can protect ourselves!"

"He's not Dracula!"

"Garlic wards off evil. Everybody knows that."

Freddie and I took off down the hall into the

kitchen. He hopped onto the counter and unhooked a whole string of garlic hanging beside the cupboards. Then he tied the ends together and slipped it over his head.

"What about me?"

"I'll protect you."

We went back to the couch. Time passed really slowly, so we turned on the TV. A news reporter was interviewing a bunch of people who looked scared. An old man talked about seeing a corpse running through his front yard. He said he called the police but they didn't find anything unusual.

The reporter turned to the camera. "Several officers on the scene suggested this sighting was most likely a Halloween prank."

"The joke's on them," I said.

We switched stations but couldn't concentrate.

"I wish I knew Greek," said Freddie.

"Why?"

"Because the corpse said something to you and I'd love to know what it was. An old Greek corpse would speak Greek, wouldn't he?"

I was so scared when the corpse grabbed my legs that I barely heard him, but now that I thought about it — "It sounded like 'parkolla'?"

"Nah," said Freddie. "It started with 'separ' like separate."

"Separkolla?"

"Something like that."

"I got it! The Greek Palace!" I shouted.

Freddie practically jumped out of his skin. "What about it?"

"Dad and I get takeout from there all the time. Somebody's *gotta* speak Greek."

"I'll get the phone book."

By the light from the TV screen, we looked up Greek Palace. I dialed, and after a couple of rings a man answered. "Um … um … I'm a student … and I'm doing an assignment for school on Greek myths."

Freddie nodded and gave me a thumbs-up.

"I was just wondering if you'd happen to know what the word 'separkolla' means in Greek?"

"I'm Portuguese," said the man. "But hold on. Maybe our waitress knows."

I heard the man talking to somebody and then a lady came on the line. "Yes, hello? What was the word you were asking about?"

"I'm not sure exactly how to pronounce it, but it kind of sounds like 'separkolla'?"

"I think you mean 'se parakalo.'"

"Se parakalo! Yes, that's it!"

Freddie rubbed his hands together and grinned. I listened while she told me what it meant.

Then I thanked her and slowly hung up the phone.

"What'd she say?"

"She said it means 'please.'"

"Why the heck would a corpse that's trying to kill you say 'please'?"

Exactly. I slowly sat down. Then it suddenly made sense. "He wasn't trying to kill me, Freddie. He was asking me for something. And the only thing he could have wanted ... is the coin."

"Ya think?"

I nodded. "It's like I told you. His soul needs it to get across the river. And I took it *back*."

"Well, he's gonna have to buy his own ticket now."

"He *can't*. A gold coin *is* the ticket."

"Hate to bring this up, Alex, but you don't *have* the coin."

"Then I'll get it back."

"*How*? I can guarantee you, saying 'please' to Slug won't work."

"I'm not going to ask him." I headed for the door.

"Do you have a death wish? He'll pound you into next week!"

"He's not home. They all left, remember?"

"Yeah. So? You gonna break in?"

"Slug's bedroom's at the back of the house —

on the ground floor. He's always bragging about how easy it is to sneak out at night."

"The window'll be *locked*!"

"Maybe not. I keep mine open."

"*Yours* is on the second floor! His will be locked. Trust me."

"Then I'll break it."

Freddie looked surprised. That didn't sound like me at all.

"What if the corpse gets you *before* you reach the window? Did ya think of that? Huh?"

"I'll run fast. It's only three houses away."

Freddie kept trying to talk me out of going, but when he realized I wouldn't change my mind, he took off his garlic necklace and slipped it over my head.

"Thanks, Freddie."

He pulled off four cloves and said if the corpse showed up, he was going to stick them in his nose and ears. "Spirits can enter your body through openings, you know."

Freddie convinced me to go to the basement with him and get a crowbar. "You might need it to pry open Slug's window."

While we were down there, I spotted a small flashlight and slipped it into my pants pocket with the cell phone. Back in the kitchen,

Freddie put the crowbar into his backpack and I slipped it on, so my hands would be free. Then we made a plan.

From Freddie's bedroom window you could see right through the two backyards between his house and Slug's. He'd watch through his binoculars, and if he saw the corpse, he'd call me on his dad's cell and tell me which way to run.

We opened the back door a crack and peeked into the yard.

"The coast is clear," whispered Freddie. "Go!"

11

I burst through the door and was across the grass in three seconds flat. The fence wasn't very high. I made it over easy, dropping down into old man Jenner's yard. His porch light was on, so I could see my way across the lawn. The fence that separated his yard from Miss Darcy's garden was a little higher. I spotted a garbage bin, stood on it and climbed over the top. Before I jumped down, I gave Freddie a little wave. I couldn't see him with the lights off, but I knew he was there watching out for me.

The huge bed sheets hanging from Miss Darcy's clothesline were blowing like crazy. It didn't make sense to me, but Miss Darcy always hung her sheets outside to dry no matter how cold it got.

The leaves crunched under my feet, but Miss Darcy is half deaf, so I didn't worry. I could see her sitting in the living room, watching TV. I wished I could be there, too. But I had to keep going.

Past the deck.

Past the barbecue.

Past the clothesline.

Then ... the cell phone rang!

I turned around, but the sheets were blowing against me and I couldn't see a thing. I yanked the phone out of my pocket. Just as I flipped it open, a shadow appeared.

"DOG! RUN!!" screamed Freddie.

The dog sprang right through the sheet!

Somehow, my legs moved and I raced toward the far fence. The dog barked wildly and snapped at my heels. "RUN, ALEX! RUN!" Freddie kept screaming.

Lucky for me there was an old patio table leaning against the fence. I leaped onto it, flung my body over the top and landed hard on the other side, rolling into a dried-out vegetable patch. I lay there, my heart pounding like crazy as the dog snarled and scratched the other side of the wooden boards.

"Alex!!" Freddie's voice yelled through the phone. "You okay?" The cell had flown out of my hand when I landed. I patted around, found it and was just about to answer when a light snapped on.

"Nelson!" Miss Darcy shouted. "Leave those squirrels alone. Come on now. Come!" Just like that, the dog stopped barking. Then I heard the sound of a patio door closing.

The light snapped off.

I waited for my heart to slow down, then told Freddie I was okay. I jammed the phone in my pocket and headed to Slug's house. There was a huge pine tree blocking the moon, but I found the window I figured was his. It had a skull and crossbones on the pane.

Freddie was right. It was locked.

I pulled the crowbar out of the backpack and worked the end between the windowsill and the frame. Pushing down hard, I heard the wood crack.

I slid the window up, crawled inside and flicked on the flashlight. What a mess! I waded through piles of clothes and made my way around the room — the coin had to be here somewhere.

I searched the nightstand, the dresser, the bookshelves and the desk. Then I remembered — Slug had put the coin in his jacket pocket. A *jean* jacket.

I checked the clothes on the floor. No jacket.

The closet!

That was an even bigger mess. I still came up empty. Where else would he put a jacket?

I made my way to the front of the house. Beside the door was a coat rack with too many coats on it. I flashed the light around and spotted the jacket dropped on a pile of shoes. When I picked it up, one side felt heavy — it had to be the money I'd given him at the restaurant.

I dumped the coins onto the floor and shone the light on them. There it was — the gold coin!

Just as I grabbed it, the front door swung open. Slug!

He flicked on the light switch and saw me with the coin in my hand. His eyes squinted really tight. "You little thief!"

I slipped past him, bolted out the door and raced by his parents. They were standing beside their car — smoke coming out of the engine. "*Alex*?" I heard Slug's dad say. I didn't stop. A second later I heard, "*Slug*?"

I leaped over some fake gravestones on Mr. Jenner's lawn and turned down Freddie's driveway to his back door. I pounded on it and shouted.

Slug came barreling around the corner. He looked really mad. I kept pounding and screaming, "Let me in! Freddie!! Let me in!"

Just as a light snapped on, Slug grabbed me. I pushed him away and took off around the garage, jumping over the legs of a ladder, but I guess Slug wasn't fast enough.

I heard a yell, then a crash. There was Slug, flat on the ground.

When I reached the porch at the back of Oddities, I scrambled over the railing and climbed our tree, yanked up the window and dove through — straight into my bedroom.

Safe!

No way Slug could climb a tree.

Thump! Something slammed against the window!

I spun around to see the top of the ladder — and Slug's face!

Heading for the door, I slipped on the carpet and went down, hard. The next thing I knew, Slug was hauling me up by the shoulders.

"I'm gonna kill you, Alex!"

I shook him off, lost my balance and fell against the dresser. Slug hunched over like a wrestler. "No one steals from me," he snarled. "*No one!*"

He lunged.

I raced for the window, but as I climbed out, he grabbed me and pulled me back inside. I hit the nightstand and went crashing to the floor.

"Okay! Okay!" I shouted. "I'll give you the coin back!"

"*Too late, squirt.*"

"What?"

"*No one steals from me.*"

Slug had really lost it. He was going to hurt me, bad. I got up and moved back but didn't get far before hitting the wall. Just as Slug raised his fist, Freddie flew through the window and landed right on top of him.

I yanked Freddie up and raced for the bedroom door. When my hand grabbed the knob, I got another huge shock.

Freddie swung the door open and pulled me through. But the hallway had disappeared again.

We went flying into the night sky.

12

Everything was black. I kicked hard but barely moved. Just when I thought my lungs would explode, I felt myself rushing upward through water. Finally, my head broke the surface. I looked around but the mist was so thick I could barely see.

"Freddie!" There was no answer. "Freddie!!"

I swam around looking for him and calling his name. Suddenly, his face popped out of the water right in front of me. He looked terrified. "Where *are* we?"

In a second, his head was underwater again. He thrashed around, screaming.

Freddie was freaking out. He coughed and gasped, then went under again. I reached over and caught his sweater. He was so panicked he grabbed me and pushed me under the water. I tried but couldn't get out from under him. Finally I just stopped moving. Freddie calmed down a little and I managed to pull away. Swimming underwater, I came up behind him. Then, flinging my arm under his chin, I pulled him onto his back.

"You're okay, Freddie. I've got you. You're okay."

After a couple of seconds, when Freddie realized he could breathe and I was holding him, his body relaxed a little. I kept repeating that everything was going to be all right. I knew it wasn't, but that's all I could think to say.

A shadow passed over us.

Looking up, we saw a huge boat floating silently through the water. It seemed to be moving in slow motion. I grabbed on to the side. Freddie grabbed on, too. The wood had some kind of carving on it, giving us good handholds. Digging our fingers in, we managed to climb up and hoist ourselves over the side as quietly as we could.

Trembling, Freddie whispered, "Where *are* we, Alex?"

I looked around. The boat was empty except for a tall, dark figure standing at the front. His back was to us. He was wearing a long cape with a hood over his head and he was rowing with a long pole.

My eyes widened. It was the same figure I'd seen from my bedroom door the other night!

"Alex?"

"I'm … I'm not sure where we are, Freddie," I whispered.

The boat suddenly pulled up onto shore.

Freddie and I peeked over the side to see where we'd landed. Standing along the water's edge were about twenty people. Well, they looked like people, only you could see right through their bodies.

"Ghosts!" Freddie yelped.

"Shhh!" I clamped my hand over his mouth and pulled him under one of the wooden benches along the side of the boat.

The figure lifted a long plank and slid it down to the sand. One at a time, the ghosts walked up the plank. When the first one got to the top, the boatman reached out his hand, palm up. The ghost dropped a coin into his hand and stepped on board. Then the second one did the same thing. That's when it hit me. The dark figure was Charon, and the ghosts were souls, paying to cross the river to the Underworld.

My blood turned to ice.

I slowly looked over at Freddie. He was so scared his body shook like crazy. I wanted to explain what was happening, but I was afraid Charon might hear us. Then what would he do? Kill us? Throw us overboard? I didn't want to find out.

I pulled Freddie deeper into the shadows, and we watched the rest of the souls step into the boat. Their faces looked really peaceful. The first soul sat on the bench across from us. We could have reached out and touched it. Not that we wanted to.

When the last soul got to the top of the plank, Charon stepped forward and blocked its way. The soul turned its palm up. It didn't have a coin. We heard it say, "Se parakalo."

"That's what our corpse said!" I whispered.

Charon shook his head, then pointed a long, gnarly finger back to the shore. Could this be the soul of the corpse at home? Looking really sad, the soul turned and walked back down the plank.

The gold coin! I could give it to him and he could get on the boat! I frantically searched my pockets.

It was gone. Probably at the bottom of the river.

My rummaging made noise and the soul sitting across from us turned his head. He looked straight at Freddie and me.

Then he smiled.

Charon pulled the plank into the boat and pushed off with the pole. We made a slow turn and headed away from the shore. With Charon busy at the front, I felt safe enough to get up and look over the edge.

The corpse's soul was standing alone on the

shore, watching us sail away. I had a feeling — no, I *knew* — this was our corpse.

I hated Charon for leaving him behind. It seemed so mean. He made enough money from the others — he could have let *one* soul on without paying. I thought about all the years our corpse's soul had been waiting, all the years he'd watched everybody else go across while he was left behind.

Suddenly, Freddie pulled me down. "What are we gonna *do*?" He looked desperate.

"I don't know."

"We gotta get back home!"

"*How?*"

"I don't *know* how! You got us into this. You get us out."

"I'll think of something, Freddie. I promise." I said it like I meant it, but I was terrified.

13

Freddie and I huddled together to get warm. "Where do you think he's taking us?" Freddie asked through chattering teeth.

From what Dad had read to me, I knew exactly where we were headed. But I couldn't tell Freddie. He was scared enough. "I don't know," was all I said.

I wondered what the Underworld would be like. Just as I had that thought, the soul sitting across from us looked at me. His mouth didn't move but I heard his voice. *The Underworld is filled with shadows. It's a place without hope, without joy, where the dead fade into nothing.*

Why would souls pay to go to a place like that?

The soul read my mind again. *One need not pay to enter the Underworld, only to cross the river. Payment is exacted by Charon in his greed.*

So souls don't really need a gold coin? I didn't say these words, just thought them.

Without Charon, how could we get across?

He had a point, I guess.

Freddie and I sat quietly for a little while. The

Underworld sure didn't sound very nice.

Noble and pure souls go on to the Elysian Fields, the soul said. *It's paradise.* A beautiful smile crossed his face.

Just then Freddie sneezed.

It wasn't very loud, but Charon must have heard it because he spun around. His face was human looking, long and thin with ugly pockmarks. His hair was straggly and his eyes glowed red. I pulled Freddie farther under the bench. There was no way Charon could see us from where he was standing, and a couple of seconds later we felt the boat moving again.

Freddie and I barely breathed till the boat slid onto the shore.

Welcome to the Underworld, the soul said, as he and the others stood up.

My stomach tightened.

Charon set the plank down and we watched from under the bench while the souls, one by one, passed him and stepped off the boat. When the last soul got off, so did he, saying, "The Messenger awaits."

The Messenger? What message did he have? I was too afraid to look.

We waited a little longer and then finally I said, "Freddie, we can't stay here."

"Yes, we *can*! We're gonna wake up any minute and be back at home. This is a bad dream, that's all."

If only he was right.

I crawled out from under the bench and peered over the side of the boat. The souls were walking, following a man — at least he looked like a man. I couldn't see through him. He was wearing a tunic and helmet, and his sandals looked like they had wings on them. He was leading the souls toward a reddish mountain range. He must be the Messenger.

I glanced around. Charon was heading away from the mountains, toward some distant rocks.

I turned and motioned for Freddie to follow me.

"Where are we going?" he asked, his voice filled with fear.

"With the souls. It's better than waiting around for Charon to kill us."

"Maybe he'll just give us a good talking-to."

"He doesn't look like the talking type."

Freddie thought about it for a second and nodded. "You're right."

We crawled over the side of the boat facing away from Charon. Then we climbed down and jumped onto the sand.

Now Charon was standing, like a statue, on top of the rocks, looking out over the water.

Freddie and I took off across the sand. It felt really soft, much softer than sand at the beach. We caught up to the souls just as they were heading into a cave. Whatever was inside had to be better than staying here with Charon.

As we went in, I looked around for the nice soul that had talked to me on the boat, but the cave was too dark.

"It is rare to see mortals in the Underworld."

My head snapped in the direction of the voice. It was the Messenger.

"Please don't tell on us!" whispered Freddie.

"Why are you so fearful?" he asked. "Fear is of the other world."

He was so casual — like it was no big deal to see us there.

When we reached the far end of the cave, the Messenger waved his arms in a circle. Suddenly, the back wall opened and we were looking at an empty gray sky. He walked through the opening and we all followed. The souls' faces looked even more peaceful, and for some reason, I didn't feel so scared anymore.

As we walked out into the dull light, we saw

these huge gates. They must have been three stories high and looked like they were made of pure white stone. "There is nothing to fear here," a soul walking next to Freddie said out loud.

"Oh yeah? What about *him*?"

Just inside the gate was a gigantic three-headed dog, almost as tall as the gates. He had long, sharp fangs and a thick, scaly dragon's tail that snapped back and forth, thumping the ground.

Freddie started making squeaking sounds. In a gentle voice, the soul said, "Cerberus guards the entrance. He will not harm you ... all may enter."

"Even mortals?" I managed to say.

"He makes no judgment."

"Let's go back, Alex!" Freddie'd found his voice.

"*Where*?"

"To the boat!"

"What if Charon's come back?"

"What if he *hasn't*!"

I tried to calm Freddie down. "You heard what the soul said. This monster dog thing lets everybody in."

"And you *believe* him?"

Just as we got to the gate, I pulled Freddie to the side.

"You don't trust him either, do you, Alex?" he said.

"It's not that."

"Then what?"

"Remember, on the boat — when the soul said you don't need a coin to get into the Underworld?"

"No. When did he say that?"

"Well, he didn't actually say it. He *thought* it and I heard him."

"You can read their minds?"

"I guess … sort of. Anyway, I think what he meant was, a soul *doesn't* need a coin to get in *here*. He just needs to pay to get across the river."

"Yeah. So?"

"So … what if *we* bring our corpse across?"

"*We?* You and *me?*"

"Who else?"

"And just *how* are we gonna do that?"

"We'll take the *boat.*"

"Are you nuts? Like Charon's just gonna hand it over?"

"I *have* to go back for him, Freddie. I'm *meant* to help him get across."

"Maybe that's what *you're* meant to do. Not *me!*"

"You're right."

"I am?" He sounded surprised.

"Stay here if you want. It's okay."

Freddie poked his head around the gate and looked at the giant three-headed dog. "Yeah, right. Like I'm gonna hang with *this* puppy."

I laughed. Freddie shook his head. "Next time Slug comes after you, I'm goin' out for a sandwich."

14

When Freddie and I got to the cave opening, there was Charon, still standing on the rocks, his back to us.

"We *can't* steal the boat with him right *there*," whispered Freddie.

"We're a lot closer to the boat than he is. If we're really quiet, we can make it without him hearing us."

"Ya think?"

I nodded.

We both took a deep breath and started tiptoeing across the sand. I kept looking at Charon but he never moved.

We shoved the plank onto the deck and pushed with our shoulders against the boat. It was really light and slid right into the water without a sound. Amazing.

We waded in, climbed up the side away from Charon, swung ourselves over the top and stepped onto a bench. Then, crouching low, we quickly moved to the front. Lifting the pole, we silently slipped it into the water. One last look —

Charon was still facing the other way. Perfect.

Then the cell phone rang!

It startled us so much we both screamed. Charon's head snapped in our direction. Even this far away we could see his blood-red eyes blazing. In a second he was off the rocks, moving incredibly fast.

"PUSH, Freddie!" I yelled. "PUSH!!"

Freddie and I pushed the pole as hard as we could. It touched bottom and the boat moved. But not very fast. It was too big. Freddie started bawling really loud, but he kept pushing.

Charon raced to the edge of the shore. I thought for sure we were toast, but as soon as his cloak touched the water, it started to burn.

"Look, Freddie!"

Freddie turned his head in time to see Charon yank his cloak out of the water and step back. "What happened?"

"I don't know! The water didn't hurt *us*!"

For some reason, Charon couldn't go in the water. We could hardly believe our luck.

The large pole wasn't easy to handle, but the trip across to the Underworld had been pretty fast, so we knew it wouldn't take long to get back.

We couldn't see Charon anymore but suddenly we heard his booming voice. "I call upon Hecate, goddess of darkness, terror of the night."

"*Where is he*?!" shrieked Freddie.

"You, who roam in moonless skies, go forth! Bring death to those who have stolen from me!"

A loud clap of thunder cracked, the sky tore open, and a woman with flowing hair came flying straight at us. Behind her were a pack of vicious, snarling wolves. Freddie and I screamed and dove flat on the deck. The wolves passed right over our heads. Following them were deep purple clouds. Soon the whole sky was dark. There was another ear-splitting crack and then rain pounded down. The river suddenly heaved as if there'd been an explosion, and the front of the boat shot up. Freddie and I were thrown back but managed to wrap our arms around a bench leg, holding on as tightly as we could. A huge wave rose and rushed into the boat.

We didn't stand a chance.

15

When we hit the water, it was like a tunnel spiraling deeper and deeper. Just when I thought for sure we were going to die, another wave rose from below us, lifting us higher and higher. Then the wall of water roared forward and hurled us onto the shore.

We lay there, unable to move, our breath loud rasps. Finally, I dragged myself up and staggered over to Freddie. "Are you all right?"

He didn't answer.

When I tried to help him up, he pulled away and yelled, "Leave me alone!" So I did.

The boat was lying on its side, half in the water. It looked like a beached whale. Farther to the right, I could see the pole jammed deep into the sand. The soul was nowhere in sight, but neither were the wolves.

I heard a groan. "You okay, Freddie?"

He groaned even louder as he tried to walk. After three steps he dropped back down on the sand. "What are we gonna do, Alex? I can't take much more."

"I'm really sorry I got you into this."

Freddie just stared at the waves lapping gently on the shore. Finally he said, "My mom must be worried sick."

I nodded.

A light went off in our heads. "The phone!"

I patted my jacket pocket. It was still there!

"I can't believe it!" said Freddie. "Did the water wreck it?"

"Looks okay to me."

"Do you think it'll go through from here?"

"It rang before."

"Yeah!" Freddie looked hopeful. "Try your house first. If they're not there, try mine."

"Okay."

"What'll you say if you reach them?"

I thought for a second. "I'll say we're okay and tell them not to worry and then, before they can ask us where we are, we'll make staticky sounds and pretend we got disconnected!"

"Sounds like a plan."

I flipped open the cover on the cell. Freddie pulled my hand away. "What if Slug told them what he saw?"

I shook my head. "They'd never believe him."

I punched in the numbers, pressed Send and held my breath. Freddie closed his eyes.

"It's ringing!"

Freddie's eyes popped open. "*Really?*"

I nodded and crossed my fingers.

"Hello?" Dad's voice sounded really anxious.

"Dad, it's me, Alex."

"Slug said you and Freddie fell through your bedroom door and disappeared!"

I looked at Freddie. "He told," I whispered.

"I *knew* he would. Hang up! Hang up!"

I panicked, but at the last second I went on the defensive. "Slug said *what*? Is he *crazy*?"

"Then where *are* you, son? And where's Freddie? We've been worried sick."

"Didn't you read the note?"

"*What* note?"

"Freddie and I got a last-minute invitation to a Halloween party. It's at …" I started to make staticky sounds. I waved to Freddie to make more sounds. He did. "Dad! Are you still there?"

"I'm here, Alex!"

"I can't hear you, Dad."

"Alex!"

"We'll talk later, okay? We won't be too late."

I pressed End and flipped the cover shut.

Freddie looked impressed. "You're good."

We knew our parents were still confused, but that was better than being worried. Now, all we had to do was find the soul and get him across the river.

But where was he?

Freddie and I walked along the beach. We saw nothing but sand.

"Maybe we're in the wrong spot."

"You might be right," I said. "But let's go a bit farther, okay?"

Our feet sank deep into the sand, making it really hard to walk. "It's hopeless," cried Freddie. "This shore could go on forever!"

"The river wasn't that wide and we got across in just a couple of minutes. How far —"

"There he is!" Freddie shouted, pointing ahead to a sandy hill.

When we got to the top, we saw *five* souls all standing peacefully, looking out over the water.

One soul was sitting. He slowly raised his head and made a wailing sound filled with pain. It cut right through us.

I walked over and knelt in front of him. The soul looked at me with the saddest eyes I'd ever seen.

"My name is Alex." I spoke softly so I wouldn't scare him. But I didn't have to worry. He wasn't scared, just sad. "This is my cousin, Freddie."

Freddie gave him a little wave.

The soul tilted his head back and wailed again. The sound filled the air, echoing in the silence.

"It's gonna be all right," I said to him. "Really. Freddie and I are here to take you across the river."

The soul's eyes still looked sad. He slowly turned his palm up to show me that nothing was inside.

"You don't *need* a coin. We'll take you across for *free*. Honest." A spark of hope seemed to appear in his eyes. "You wait here, okay? Do you understand? Just wait here and we'll go get the boat."

I don't know if he believed us or not, but it didn't matter. "Come on, Freddie," I said. And we took off.

When we got to the boat, we realized there was no way we could lift it upright. "It's way too big, Alex!"

Think. Think.

I noticed some dead fish floating on the water. Then it hit me. "Freddie!"

"What?"

"We don't have to *lift* the boat, we just have to *push* it … into the water!"

I was right. When we pushed hard, the boat

started to move. After about a minute, it was completely in the water right side up. We cheered and hugged each other.

"Climb in, Freddie, I'll go get the pole."

Freddie climbed along the ridges and jumped into the boat. I pulled the pole out of the sand, ran back and handed it to him, then climbed up, too. It only took a few minutes to get to where the soul was sitting. When we landed, Freddie and I found the plank jammed under a bench and slid it to the sand.

The corpse's soul stared at us. "C'mon," I said, waving my arm for him to come aboard. "It's okay. Really."

He didn't seem very sure, but finally he walked over and stepped onto the plank. Slowly, he made his way up. When he got to the top, I smiled and Freddie motioned for him to sit on a bench. He was afraid to step into the boat. When he looked at me again, I nodded.

He stepped in and sat on the first bench, glancing around like he couldn't believe this was really happening. Then he started to cry. After a few moments he stopped, looked at me and smiled. My heart almost burst with happiness.

I turned to pull in the plank but the other souls were walking along it. "Freddie?"

"Yeah?"

"They're coming."

Freddie moved over to me. "Do you think we'd be breaking some rule if we let them come along?"

We looked at each other and then both said, "Who cares?"

The first soul stretched out his hand to give me his gold coin. "No, no. It's okay. You can come on free."

Freddie's hand shot out. He took the coin, grinned and said, "Welcome aboard. Come right on in. Make yourself comfortable."

The soul stepped into the boat. Then the next and the next, until all five were in. "Take any seat," said Freddie. "Any seat at all. They all have a great view." Then he jingled the gold coins in his hand and smiled.

Freddie and I pushed the pole into the water and started across the river. We decided to veer off a little so that when we arrived on the other side, it wouldn't be where we'd left Charon.

The air was clear and clean. It made us feel stronger. The river was calm, and the only sound was when the pole pushed down through the water. Until Freddie's stomach growled. "Man, I'm hungry," he said. "I should have had more spaghetti for supper."

"Is there any food in your backpack?"

"Hey! Yeah!"

I slipped off Freddie's backpack and unzipped it. Water poured out. Reaching in, I found two soggy sandwiches. "Sorry, Freddie."

"I'm not hungry enough to eat *that*," he said. "Give 'em to the fish."

I took the plastic wrap off and threw the sandwiches into the river.

"Is there anything else in there?" Freddie asked.

"Just the crowbar and ... wait a minute." I held up some grapes. "Ta-dum!"

"You take the pole while I — What was *that*?" Something was moving under the boat — something big.

I leaned over the side. "There's a shadow down there," I whispered, "and the sandwiches are gone."

"You shouldn't have thrown them in!"

"You told me to!"

Freddie pulled in the pole. "What do you think it is?" he asked, stepping over to me to get a look. A dark mass circled slowly around the boat.

"I've never seen a fish *this* big."

I tossed the grapes back in the backpack and yanked out the crowbar. Gripping it tightly, I held it over my head, the sharp end forward.

"What good's that gonna do?" Freddie screamed.

"I dunno, but it's all we've got!"

Whatever it was stayed for a while and then moved off.

Freddie and I stared at the water. Our bodies were shaking so hard neither of us could speak. But the souls — their faces were still peaceful. I guess you're not afraid of dying when you're already dead.

Freddie grabbed the pole and pushed hard. Less than five minutes later, our boat landed on the soft sand of the Underworld.

16

I tucked the crowbar into the backpack. "We might still need this."

Freddie slipped the pack on. Then we both lifted the plank to let the souls off. The Messenger was nowhere in sight, but we headed off, keeping our eyes open for Charon.

"I sure hope we're going in the right direction," said Freddie.

Our feet were sinking so deeply in the sand we were exhausted. I turned to see how the souls were doing. They were walking on *top* of the sand, as calm as ever.

Just when Freddie and I thought we couldn't go another step, he pointed. "The rocks!"

There, just ahead, were the rocks where Charon had stood. He wasn't there.

"Whew!"

"The cave opening's gotta be around here someplace," Freddie muttered.

"There it is!" I said.

"Come on, everybody!" Freddie waved for the souls to follow him.

"Wait!"

Freddie stopped. "What's wrong?"

"If Charon's not on the beach, maybe he's *in* the cave."

"Right. A trap. What are we gonna do?"

"I've got an idea."

I walked over to our corpse's soul. He smiled. "Freddie and I need your help."

"What can I do for you?"

I pointed to the cave opening. "To get to the gates that lead to the Underworld, we have to go through that cave. I think the souls will be all right, but Freddie and I might not be. Not if Charon's in there. He's mad at us for stealing his boat."

"You wish me to check?"

"Yes. Please."

"It is small payment for what you have done for me."

We watched as the soul walked into the cave — and came out again. "It is safe."

Freddie and I breathed a sigh of relief. Then we all went inside.

"How do we get through to the other side, Alex?"

"The Messenger just waved his arms and it opened."

Freddie started waving. Nothing happened. He changed to a flapping motion, like some giant bird.

The wall opened.

"Hey, look at that!" he said, laughing.

The Messenger stepped into the cave. He must have opened it from the other side. We could tell he was surprised to see us and even more surprised to see the souls. "I was not aware there would be others today." His voice was friendly. "But all are welcome. Come."

The souls followed the Messenger, and Freddie and I followed them. Suddenly, our bodies were picked up and flung back into the cave. We were staring into blazing red eyes.

"No one steals from me," said Charon in a deep, evil voice. "No one!"

Slug's exact words!

"Freddie!" I shouted. "Give him the coins!"

"But ..."

"Now!!"

"Okay!" Freddie jammed his hand into his pocket and pulled out the coins. He was about to put them into Charon's outstretched hand but, at the last second, he spun around and threw them toward the mouth of the cave. In a lightning-fast motion, Charon leaped for the coins.

As the cave wall started to close, I grabbed Freddie and hurled him through the opening. I dove through just in time.

Charon flew right at us. But the wall closed in his face.

"Quick thinking, Freddie."

He looked proud of himself. "Thanks."

We turned toward the gates to the Underworld. The Messenger and the souls were already passing through, paying no attention to the giant three-headed dog, who was still whipping his dragon tail around.

"He doesn't look too friendly," said Freddie.

"I know. But remember, 'All are welcome.'"

"Then what's he *doing* here?"

"Who knows? Let's just go past *really* carefully."

We edged around him, sticking close to the rock wall of the huge gate. The dog barely noticed — then we walked right in.

The light got duller inside — everything was gray. Trees, rocks, sand, even the air. All the color had been sucked out, like in a picture I saw once of a city hit by an atom bomb.

We looked around. No souls. Which way did they go?

In the distance we spotted a large pyramid.

"Do you think they're in there?" Freddie asked.

"Could be."

When we got to it, we walked around the whole building but couldn't find a door.

"How can there be no door?" Freddie looked really confused.

"Maybe in the Underworld they don't need doors."

I reached out to touch the wall and my hand went right through it. Freddie caught me before I fell.

"Whoa!"

"If my arm went in, our whole bodies probably can, too," I said.

"You try first."

I closed my eyes and walked straight ahead. When I opened my eyes again, I was inside. Freddie followed, banging into me.

A laser show was on. Beautiful colors were shooting into the air. There was music, too. It was awesome.

When the show was finally over, we saw marble steps leading to a huge stage. Three men dressed in golden robes sat on thrones. They looked like kings.

In front of the kings stood one of the souls that Freddie and I had brought across the river. He was holding one end of a long thread — the rest was in a huge pile on the floor.

The king on the middle throne stood up and in a deep voice said, "Tolas Mellinius, as reward for the exemplary life you have lived, it is my *great* honor to send you on to the Elysian Fields."

Bells rang, filling the room with a wonderful sound. Out of thin air, a Being materialized. It had the shape of a man but it was all light. Stretching out its arm, it said, "Follow me."

The soul did. Within a few steps they both rose into the air and disappeared.

"Wow!" Freddie said.

The other souls were waiting at the bottom of the stairs — our corpse's soul first in line. I spotted the Messenger standing near us. "Are those guys kings?" I whispered.

"They are judges called the Ancient Ones."

The judge in the middle raised his scepter and gently said, "Costas Arianos, you may advance."

Costas. So that was his name.

Two escorts walked him up the nine steps to the stage. The judge waved his scepter again and a huge tapestry unrolled in front of Costas. It hovered in mid-air. Costas reached out and pulled a thread at the bottom. As it unraveled, bright, colorful lights — brilliant greens, reds, yellows and blues — shot out. The laser show began again. An otherworldly music played and I swear I heard laughter.

The lights followed the line of the thread as it unwound. It was so beautiful I felt like crying. I looked at Freddie. His cheeks were shiny with tears.

Then the thread suddenly stopped.

So did the lights and the music.

A small flame burned through the thread and it dropped to the floor. The thread had stopped at a black circle.

"What happened?" Freddie whispered in surprise.

The Messenger leaned in. "That is the tapestry of his life. The bright colors are the good he has done, the black circle an evil he committed."

Evil?

Just then a large round mirror came out of the floor. It was all cloudy, but when it cleared, we saw a baby sleeping in a crib. A figure appeared, but we could only see it from the back. The figure walked slowly to the crib, leaned over the baby and yanked off its blanket.

"I can't look," cried Freddie, spinning around so fast he banged into me. I stumbled back against a pillar. The Messenger grabbed me.

"Sorry," whispered Freddie. "You okay?"

"I did not harm that baby!" Costas's voice echoed through the hall.

The judge looked at him. "We are responsible not only *for* our actions, but also for the *outcome* of those actions. So it has been decreed by the gods."

"I am innocent!"

"Your actions put into motion events that led directly to the death of the firstborn child of King Talasius."

Costas looked horrified. "It cannot be!"

"Costas Arianos." The judge slowly raised his scepter. "It is my sad duty to condemn you to Tartarus, the Chamber of Darkness."

Freddie and I looked at each other. "Chamber of Darkness?"

"There you will be held in containment for all eternity."

A strong wind whipped through the room. The thread flew into the air, spinning in circles. Two guards appeared and stood on either side of Costas.

The judge said, "Walk the Path of Death."

"NO!" wailed Costas. "NOOOOO!"

Just then Costas looked right at me. How did he know I was there? His tortured eyes burned into mine. Then he and the guards vanished.

I turned to Freddie. "He's innocent! He didn't *do* anything!"

When the wind stopped, the tapestry thread was near my feet. As I gathered it up and looked at the beautiful colors, I knew Costas was telling the truth.

I had to help him.

17

The Messenger must have read my mind. "Find the oracle, Tiresias," he said. "He is wise and knows things that other men do not. Perhaps he can help you."

"Where is he?"

"In the Elysian Fields."

Freddie frowned. "Where's that?"

The Messenger thought for a moment and then said, "I will lead you to the entrance."

The next thing we knew, we were outside, walking along a wide dirt path. After the incredible light shows, the grayness seemed even gloomier.

"Are the Elysian Fields far?" Freddie asked.

"Nothing is far in the Underworld."

"What's an oracle?" I added.

"Someone who can both see the past and predict the future."

"Tiresias can do that?"

"That and much more."

"When did he die?" I asked.

"He is not dead," said the Messenger. "He is

mortal, like you."

"How's that possible?"

"With the gods, all things are possible."

"Doesn't this Tiresias guy feel a little out of place?" asked Freddie. "With all the souls, I mean."

"He has become accustomed."

"If he isn't dead," I asked, "what's he doing in the Underworld?"

The path we were on began going down a hill.

"Many years ago, Hades, the god of the Underworld, abducted the beautiful Persephone and brought her to his palace to be his wife. She begged to be allowed to return to her family. Hades told her she could go, but first offered her the seed of a pomegranate to ease her hunger. By eating it she became bound to remain in Hades."

"Because she ate one little seed?" Freddie was amazed.

"The amount does not matter. It is a rule. One may leave only if one has not eaten while there."

"But he doesn't tell anybody the rule, right?" I asked.

"Correct."

"What a *sneak*!" Now Freddie was getting mad.

The Messenger smiled. "Tiresias, the oracle you seek, came to the Underworld to try to rescue Persephone. He was caught and, as punishment, was forced to remain forever."

"Even though he wasn't *dead*?"

"Yes."

Freddie shook his head. "Talk about bad luck."

"Tiresias is fortunate in one way. He is allowed to live in the Elysian Fields. And it is truly a paradise."

"Where the souls that were really good in life go?"

"Correct. It is also the place where heroes go."

"Cool." Freddie's eyes brightened. "Maybe I can get an autograph!"

At a fork in the road the Messenger turned right. I glanced back and noticed the grass and trees along the left fork were all dead and shriveled. "Where does the other road lead?" I asked.

"To the realm ruled by Hades."

As we walked along, the air around us grew lighter and the gray sky turned a pale blue. I started feeling lighter, too — and stronger. A few minutes later, the road came to an end. We stood at the edge of a great forest of tall trees with long, deep green leaves that looked like velvet. The Messenger stepped into the forest. We followed him.

A couple of minutes later, we stopped at the opening of a long laneway. A straight row of trees lined each side, their trunks curving inward and their branches joining at the top. It created a beautiful archway.

"I leave you here," said the Messenger. "Simply walk through and you will find yourselves in the Elysian Fields."

"You're gonna leave us here *alone*?" Freddie sounded worried.

"The shades await me."

I frowned. "Shades?"

"The souls of the dead. More have gathered at the river and I must escort them to judgment."

"Please don't go!" cried Freddie.

The Messenger smiled and said, "You have the hearts of heroes. I wish you well on your journey."

With that, he turned, walked a few steps and disappeared.

Freddie and I looked at each other. "Heroes?" We both grinned.

Taking a deep breath, we started down the laneway.

Shafts of soft blue light shone through the branches. As we went farther along, the light kept getting brighter. At the end of the lane, we found ourselves looking out over a gorgeous meadow.

The grass was past our ankles and greener

than anything we'd ever seen. It waved in the cool breeze and glistened like it was covered in dew. And the sky! It was the most incredible turquoise and seemed to stretch on forever.

We heard singing. Where was it coming from? It sounded like a choir. The sound filled us with such happiness and peace, we couldn't stop smiling.

Suddenly, out of nowhere, we were surrounded by butterflies, their colorful wings glittering in the sunlight as they danced around us.

"This *can't* be real!" Freddie's eyes were as big as saucers.

Dozens of butterflies landed — on our bodies and in our hair. The others flew off toward a small hill dotted with red poppies. "Let's go," I said. "Maybe they're on the other side."

Freddie just kept looking at all the butterflies on him and smiling ear to ear. I had to pull his arm to get him moving.

We quickly reached the hill, climbed to the top and looked down.

What we saw made our jaws drop.

There were *thousands* of souls. They kind of looked like the Being made of light back in the pyramid except that the light from these souls was shimmering.

"Pinch me, Alex. I gotta be dreaming."

Freddie was right. It *was* like a wonderful dream.

The longer we stayed, the happier we felt. It was like every breath we took energized us.

"I'm gonna start floating any second," Freddie said. "If I do, don't stop me, okay?"

"Okay, but don't float too far."

We stood there watching as souls talked together. When they moved, little streaks of color, like mini-rainbows, trailed behind them. Some were eating at long tables covered with the most delicious-looking food, others were lying on the grass listening to music.

Somehow we started walking. All the souls we passed smiled at us. "Boy, they're friendly here," said Freddie, waving at them like he was in a parade. "How ya doin'? Nice to see ya."

After a while we came to a courtyard. I looked around at the souls there. "I wonder where Tiresias is."

"Who cares?" Freddie kept waving.

I understood how Freddie felt. Nothing seemed to matter. It all just felt so good. I had to force myself to remember why we'd come. "We're here to help Costas. Remember?"

"Costas. Oh yeah."

"Tiresias has to be around here somewhere."

One of the souls must have heard me because he turned and said, "Tiresias is at the fountain."

"Could you tell us which way that is, please?"

He stretched out his shimmering arm and pointed.

"Thank you."

Freddie and I made our way through a grove of trees and soon found ourselves in a park. I swear it looked almost like the park at home, only there was a huge crystal fountain in the middle spraying water high in the air. There were lots of souls standing around it.

"How will we know which one's Tiresias?" Freddie asked as we headed for the fountain.

"That's easy," I said. "He's mortal."

"How can I help you?"

We spun around. The voice belonged to a man with white hair, a curly white beard and a kind face. He was wearing a robe tied at the waist.

"Are you Tiresias?" I asked.

"I am."

"We're mortals, too!" said Freddie.

Tiresias smiled. "I see that. It is not often mortals find their way to the Underworld."

"We sort of fell into it," I said. "Not really sure how."

"Perhaps someone called you."

"Called?"

"It happened to me."

Just then Freddie's stomach growled. "Sorry, but I'm *starving*." He looked embarrassed. "I could sure use a burger."

"Burgers won't be invented for another couple of thousand years," I said.

"I can provide you with that which you seek," said Tiresias to Freddie.

"A *ham*burger?"

"Yes."

"*How*?"

"Tell me what century you are from."

"The twenty-first."

Tiresias nodded, then reached his arm into the air. It disappeared right up to his elbow. A second later, his arm reappeared holding a burger.

"You gotta be kidding me!" Freddie couldn't believe what he was seeing.

"I kid you not," said Tiresias.

Freddie took the burger. "This is *unbelievable*! How'd you *do* that?"

"Parallel time," said Tiresias. "Past, present and future are all simultaneous, merely in different dimensions. Through a tear in the fabric of time, you can step into any age ... if you know how."

"You are so cool!" said Freddie between bites.

While Freddie ate his burger, I turned to Tiresias. "We came to ask for your help."

He nodded. "I know."

"You know what happened to Costas?"

"I do. And he speaks the truth. He had no knowledge of the murder of the little prince."

"*Prince?*" Freddie looked surprised.

"The son of King Talasius, remember?" I said.

"Upon discovering his murdered body, the king went mad," said Tiresias. "His throne passed to his brother, Prince Dameon."

"Did his brother know about the murder?"

"He ordered it."

Freddie and I looked at each other, confused. I turned back to Tiresias. "If Prince Dameon ordered it, why was Costas sentenced to the Chamber of Darkness?"

"Punishment in the Underworld is not only for one's actions but for *outcomes* of those actions."

That's what the judge in the pyramid had said.

"What did he do that got the baby murdered?"

"He stole the Eternal Flame."

"What's that?" asked Freddie, licking mayonnaise off his fingers.

"It is a flame that burns in the Sacred Hearth of every Greek village. It is inextinguishable."

"Why's it so important?"

"Because without it, the ritual naming of newborn children cannot be performed. If they are not named, they are not received into the family of man. To die without a name dooms one's soul to roam the earth forever."

"I can't believe Costas would steal something *that* important," I said.

"He did so innocently."

"How can you steal and be innocent?"

"He meant no harm. It was an initiation challenge."

"Initiation into what?"

"A secret society — an elite club that many young men wished to join. Only by knowing a member was there any chance of getting in."

Tiresias bent over the pool at the base of the fountain. "Allow me to show you." He slowly passed his hand over the water. Ripples flowed outward. Then a picture appeared — sort of like the mirror in the pyramid. At first we could only make out dark shapes, but gradually the image got clearer.

Two guys walked toward a black door. One was blindfolded. The other one knocked three times, waited, then knocked three times again. The door slowly opened and they went inside a room. More guys, maybe seventeen or eighteen years old, sat on chairs in a circle. One chair was bigger. The guy sitting in it asked, "You wish to join our society?"

"I do," replied the blindfolded man.

"Are you willing to perform the initiation challenge, whatever it may be?"

"I am."

"Good." He leaned back in his chair. "To join, each new member must commit a crime. This crime becomes his secret and we, his loyal brothers, keep this secret with him. That is the bond we have." He waited for a second before continuing. "Once one has been initiated, he may never leave the society. Should he attempt to do so, his secret will be revealed. Do you understand?"

"I do."

"Costas Arianos, your initiation challenge is to steal the Eternal Flame from the Sacred Hearth of Hestia. We will keep the flame for one day and then return it to the hearth. Do you agree to do this deed?"

Costas didn't answer.

"Do you agree?" repeated the leader. His voice sounded hard.

"I … I do."

The images in the water disappeared. Tiresias stood and said, "A week later, King Talasius's son was born, but the flame had not been returned. Costas realized he had been deceived. He set out to confess his crime to the king and to commit himself to returning the Eternal Flame. But before he reached the palace, he was murdered."

"That's *terrible*," said Freddie.

"Costas was trying to do the right thing!" I felt my anger rising. "Don't the judges know that?"

"In the Underworld, it is not *intentions* but *actions* that are rewarded or punished."

"What kind of justice is *that*?" I was furious. "Costas doesn't deserve to be punished for a murder he didn't commit!"

"As I told you," said Tiresias calmly, "it is both one's actions *and* their consequences that matter."

"Then let's change the action! You said past, present and future are all happening at the same time. If that's true, we can go to Greece through that tear in the fabric thing you talked about, find the flame and return it. That'll change the outcome!"

Tiresias shook his head. "We cannot perform the action. It is not our destiny."

"You mean ... only Costas can?"

Tiresias nodded.

I took a deep breath. "Then we have to go get him."

Freddie's eyes opened wide. "Are you *nuts*? He's in the Chamber of *Darkness*!"

"Sorry, Freddie. But I have to."

"Well *I* don't." He sat on the edge of the fountain. "I'm staying right here, thank you very much."

Tiresias turned to Freddie. "You are free to do as you choose."

"Good, because I choose to stay. See ya. Adios. Hasta la vista. I'll hang with the shades, listen to a little music, eat a little food."

"The food of the Underworld does not satisfy the living," said Tiresias.

"No food?"

Tiresias shook his head.

"How long d'ya think you'll be gone?" Freddie sounded a bit nervous.

"It may be some time," said Tiresias.

Freddie thought hard. "If I come, will you do your disappearing arm thing and get me a milk shake once in a while?"

Tiresias smiled. "It will be my pleasure."

18

Freddie and I followed Tiresias through the green grass of the Elysian Fields and soon found ourselves back on the road. As we walked along, Tiresias explained that the tapestry of life *can* be changed, "Although it rarely happens. If the thread is pulled during a certain time in a person's life, and that part is unraveled, one can go back and change it. Once it has been changed, the tapestry is restitched."

"Who stitches it?" asked Freddie.

"Each person has an accompanying spirit whose purpose is to create the tapestry of that life as it is lived."

"Then my tapestry is being stitched right now?"

"As we speak, my friend. So choose your actions carefully. Nothing goes unrecorded."

When we got to the fork in the road, Freddie's stomach growled again. He looked over at Tiresias. "A cola and large fries, please."

Tiresias put his arm through the air.

"Oh, and an apple turnover!" Freddie added. "Two! Two turnovers!"

Tiresias's arm disappeared and three seconds later, he was holding a takeout bag. "I told them it was to go." He smiled.

"You're *too* much, Tiresias!"

Freddie grabbed the bag, yanked it open and lifted out the drink and fries. He offered me and Tiresias some but we said no. I tucked the bag with the turnovers into his backpack for later.

We turned down the fork with the withered trees. The farther along we went, the heavier I began to feel. All the lightness and happiness I'd felt in the Elysian Fields slipped away.

"How far is the Chamber of Darkness?" Freddie asked, popping another fry into his mouth.

"If you dropped a hammer it would fall for nine days before it reached the chamber."

"Nine days! I gotta get home *way* before that or my mom will kill me!"

Tiresias smiled. "I know a shortcut. Through Hades."

"Hades?" I gulped. "You mean, hell?"

"No, no. 'Hades' merely means 'place of the dead,' not a fiery furnace. Those sent to Hades have not led a particularly bad life, but not a particularly good life, either. If they lied or cheated or stole, that is where they are sent. For a while, anyway."

"They don't have to stay forever?" I asked, surprised.

"They may choose, after a time, to go back to the world and make up for their errors."

"Sort of like getting a second chance," said Freddie.

"In a manner of speaking."

We walked on silently, Freddie munching all the way.

"Be warned," said Tiresias, "when we arrive in Hades, do not eat so much as a morsel of food."

"Why not?"

I looked at Freddie. "Don't you remember what happened to Persephone?"

"Oh yeah. If you eat, you can't leave."

"That's the rule," said Tiresias. "Hades makes no exceptions."

The farther we went, the thicker the trees beside the road got. Then I heard a low moan, like someone was hurt. Out of the corner of my eye, I saw shadows. And they were moving — right along with us!

When I turned to look, there was nothing there except gray trees. But when I looked back at the road, I saw them again, long and black.

"Freddie," I whispered, "something's here."

"Where?"

"They are shades," said Tiresias. "Just keep walking."

Suddenly, I felt something on my back. It was soft at first but then I felt more pressure.

"Beware," said Tiresias. "Some shades may try to pass through."

"Through what?" I asked, my throat tightening.

"Through your body. They wish to feel your life force."

The pressure got stronger. My heart began to race. I spun around shouting, "Get away from me!"

Freddie stopped cold. "No one's there, Alex!"

"Don't you *see* them?"

Freddie looked all around. Then he must have spotted one. "Over there!" I looked where he was pointing. It was gone. "I swear! I saw something!" he yelled.

"They will not harm you," said Tiresias calmly. "They simply hunger for life." He started walking a little faster. "We must keep moving."

The shades snaked around the tree trunks, following along beside us, but none of them came onto the road the rest of the way.

Finally, off in the distance, we saw the palace of Hades. It was huge with tall marble columns and a black dome.

"Once we are inside the palace," said Tiresias, "Hades will want us to stay."

"We *can't* stay," I said. "We have to get Costas."

"We will get to your friend, but be prepared for a challenge first."

"What kind of challenge?"

"That is yet to be seen."

There were no guards at the gate. We walked right in. But the second we were inside, Freddie and I felt like heavy weights had landed on our shoulders. We could barely walk. Hundreds of souls shuffled by in a gray mist, their eyes looking down at the ground. The farther in we went, the weaker we felt.

"I think I'm gonna pass out," I whispered.

"Me, too," said Freddie.

"You are absorbing the despair of the shades that reside here," said Tiresias. "You must fight this feeling."

"How?" I asked.

"Push it away — with your mind."

I tried to hold my head up and think positive thoughts, but it wasn't easy.

Just then Hades appeared. He was bald and was wearing a long black robe. "Welcome to my home, Tiresias," he said in a hearty voice. "To what do I owe the pleasure of this visit?"

"We wish safe passage to Tartarus, my lord."

"Tartarus?" He sounded surprised. "For what purpose?"

"To contact a shade there."

Hades nodded. "Follow me."

Freddie whispered, "That was easy."

We went down a long stone hallway then entered a huge room. It was completely empty. At the far end were two doors. One was made of dark wood and had iron latches. It reminded me of the kind of door you see leading to dungeons. The other was made of gold, decorated with silver vines and leaves.

"One door leads directly to Tartarus," said Hades.

"Which one?" I asked.

He grinned. "That is for you to discover."

"How?" asked Freddie.

"What manner of fool are you? Just open them!"

That sounded too easy — there had to be a catch. "One leads to Tartarus," I said. "Where does the other one go?"

Hades smiled. "The other is a portal to the labyrinth."

I looked at Tiresias. He was staring straight ahead.

"Within the labyrinth," continued Hades, "is housed the Mirror of Evil."

"Uh-oh," Freddie said under his breath.

"A mirror that shows the faces of those mortals who devote themselves to the powers of darkness."

I didn't like the sound of *this*.

"You." Hades looked directly at me.

Freddie pushed my arm. "He means you, Alex."

"*Me?*"

"You are the leader, are you not?"

"Yup," said Freddie. "That's him. He's the leader."

I shot him a dirty look.

"If you choose the door to Tartarus," continued Hades, "you are free to pass through. But if you choose the portal, you and your friend must go into the labyrinth and return with the mirror."

I looked at Tiresias again. He didn't move a muscle — just kept staring straight ahead.

"Do you accept the challenge?"

I swallowed hard.

"… Yes."

"Then proceed."

"What about Tiresias? Can't he come with us?"

"He knows the tricks," smiled Hades. "And that wouldn't be fair now, would it?"

"*What* tricks?" whispered Freddie.

I shrugged.

"Oh," said Hades. "I forgot to mention one thing."

Now what?

"If you fail, Tiresias must remain here with me."

"*Why?*" I asked.

"I'm tired of the quality of shade the judges send to me. Nothing but dregs. An intelligent and respected man such as Tiresias will be a welcome addition."

Tiresias couldn't have been too happy about that part of the deal, but he didn't say a word. "What if we can't *get* the mirror?" I whispered to him. "You shouldn't be punished. It isn't fair."

"Then you must succeed."

I turned to Hades. "If we don't get the mirror, *we'll* stay."

Freddie's eyes bugged out. "What do you mean, *we?*"

Hades laughed. "Whatever would I do with such boring little mortals?"

"Hey," said Freddie, "who you calling boring?"

"Quiet, before I squash you like a fly."

Freddie zipped his lips with his fingers.

"Alex," said Tiresias, "this is an opportunity to help you liberate an innocent soul. It is a price I am willing to pay, no matter what the outcome."

I thought about it for a few seconds and then told Hades I was ready. "But can I talk to Freddie privately for a minute?"

Hades gave a little nod.

I grabbed Freddie's arm and pulled him to one side. "Which door do you think I should pick?"

"That's easy. The dungeon door. The gold one's too beautiful to lead to the Chamber of Darkness."

"Wouldn't he figure we'd think that? What if he switched them around?"

Freddie glanced over at Hades. "He looks pretty smart to me. Maybe he did do a switcheroo."

"Okay. I go for the gold one."

"Right."

"We're ready," I announced.

"Then proceed."

Freddie and I started walking toward the doors. Suddenly he grabbed me and pulled me back.

"*What*?"

"Alex, I still think it's the dungeon door!"

"Why?"

"Because it makes sense. Dungeons lead to bad places!"

"What about it being too obvious?"

"That's just it! It's so obvious *nobody* would pick it!"

"Good point. Okay. We go through the dungeon door."

"Good."

We started walking again. Just as we got to the doors, Freddie whispered, "What if I'm *wrong*?" We stopped. "We need another time-out!" he shouted. Then we went into a huddle.

"It's okay," I said. "You're *not* wrong. He's trying to psych us out with the gold door, but we're not buying it."

"So we go for the dungeon door?"

I nodded. "The dungeon door."

We straightened our shoulders and took a deep breath, then I swung the door open.

A blast of black light shot out and we were sucked through the portal.

19

Freddie and I crash-landed and rolled down a steep hill. Screaming at the top of our lungs, we went faster and faster until we slammed against a high hedge.

"Wrong door," Freddie whimpered. "Next time, don't listen to me."

We pulled twigs out of our hair and clothes, then looked up at the hedge. The labyrinth was as tall as a house. "Wow!" exclaimed Freddie. "I was picturing a maze like mice go through to get a piece of cheese."

"I'll bet to the mouse it looks pretty big."

"Yeah, but at least mice can *smell* the cheese. How are we ever gonna find a mirror in here?"

"And even if we do," I said, "how are we ever going to find our way back out?"

"I bet Tiresias knows how to get *out*."

"That's probably why he wasn't allowed to come."

We made our way to the entrance. It was wide enough for six people to walk in side by side. I stuck my head through and looked around. So did Freddie. There was only one path. It led off to the right. "I sure wish I'd read more of the books Dad brought home on ancient Greece. There might have been something about labyrinths in them."

"Too bad we couldn't just call the library. Miss Howard at the information desk knows *everything*."

"Freddie! You're brilliant!"

"What? What'd I say?"

I pulled out the cell phone. "If it worked once …"

"No way libraries are open *this* late."

"I'm not calling the library." I punched in some numbers.

"Who? Who're you calling?"

"The smartest person in our class."

"Rosalie?"

I nodded, then pressed Send. Please go through. *Please.*

There was a long silence and then — "It's ringing!" I could hardly believe it. After four rings, Rosalie's dad answered, sounding sleepy. I told him who I was and apologized for calling so late. He asked if I knew what time it was. Was this call really necessary? Couldn't it wait till tomorrow? I thought he'd never stop. I explained this was really, really important and promised I'd never call this late again and could he, just this once, *please* let me talk to Rosalie?

He grumbled and finally said, "Hold on."

About a minute later, Rosalie picked up the phone. "I've got it, Dad." I heard the other phone hang up. "Hello?"

"Rosalie, this is Alex. I need your help."

"What's wrong?"

"Can't explain right now, sorry. But I will when I get back."

"Back from where?"

"You wouldn't believe me if I told you."

"Fine. Keep it a secret." I heard her yawn. "What do you want, Alex?"

"Could you look something up on the Internet for me?"

"You're kidding, right?"

"Rosalie, just trust me? I really need some information right *now*. It's a matter of life or death."

"Whose? Are you in trouble?"

"Will you help me or not?"

I must have sounded desperate because she said, "It'll take a minute to boot."

"Thanks, Rosalie."

I turned to Freddie. "She's gonna help."

When Rosalie came back on the line, she said, "Okay, what do you want me to look up?"

"Key in 'Greek mythology.'"

"Greek *mythology*?"

"Yes, Rosalie. Please?"

She repeated it as she keyed it in.

"Then 'labyrinth.'"

"Lab-y-rinth. Okay, give it a sec."

Freddie and I waited anxiously. Finally I heard Rosalie say, "There are a lot of sites. What exactly are you looking for?"

"Just click the first one and see what it says."

We waited again. "It says, 'Labyrinths were complicated networks of paths and hedges creating a giant puzzle. There are trick corners and blind alleys.'"

"Go to the next one, Rosalie."

"Okay. Theseus in the Labyrinth."

"That sounds good. What does it say?"

She read silently for a minute. "It talks about this guy named Theseus whose dad begged him not to go into the labyrinth but he was determined to go anyway. Wanted to prove he was a hero or something. Then it says King Minos's daughter fell in love with him and offered to make sure he could get out of the labyrinth in return for marrying her."

"That's good! Keep going."

"Um … she knew there was only one way out, so she gave Theseus a ball of string and told him to tie it to the entrance of the labyrinth and unwind it as he went in. Then all he had to do was follow the string back out."

I couldn't believe what I was hearing. "Thank you, Rosalie. Thank you!"

"Did that help?"

"Yes! Thank you! I love you!"

Freddie's eyes bulged. I couldn't believe I'd said that. I slammed the cover down, hard.

"What'd she say?"

"I didn't give her a chance."

"No. I mean about the labyrinth."

"Oh, oh, the labyrinth. Um … she told me how we can get out of it."

"How?"

"With string. We tie one end to the branches at the entrance and unwind it as we go! Then, we just follow it out!"

Freddie frowned. "And where exactly are we gonna get string?"

I reached into my pocket and pulled out the thread from Costas's tapestry.

"Way to go, Alex!"

Freddie and I picked our way through the

mess of thread to find an end. It took forever, but finally we found it and tied it tightly to a branch at the entrance. Then we walked into the labyrinth, unwinding the thread as we went in.

"Piece of cake." Freddie grinned.

We marched right along, feeling like the two smartest guys in the world. Round and round we went, deeper and deeper into the labyrinth. Sometimes the path went left, sometimes right, up steps and down, around corner after corner. Whenever it led to a dead end, we just back-tracked along the thread and took another route.

In less than fifteen minutes, we found ourselves standing in a large grassy square. "We made it!" we both shouted. Then Freddie did a happy dance.

I dropped the thread and looked around.

There were dozens of openings along the hedge and they all looked *exactly* alike. It was a good thing we had that thread because we would never have been able to figure out which opening led out of the labyrinth.

Standing at the far end of the square was a large flat-topped stone with steps leading up to it. On the stone was a podium, like the one the school principal stands behind during assembly. It was slanted away from us. "Ten to one the mirror's on the podium," I said.

We ran over to it, bolted up the steps and circled around. There it was! It looked like an ordinary mirror with a black frame. "Do you want to look into it?" I asked Freddie.

"Yeah … No! … Yeah."

I lifted the mirror. It didn't reflect our faces, just the hedge behind us. Freddie waved his hand in front of it. Nothing. Then a lady's face appeared. We both gasped. The lady was pretty, with wavy brown hair, and she was laughing. We could actually *hear* her.

"She doesn't look evil to me," said Freddie.

Another face came through. This time it was a teenage boy. His face was red and he looked really angry. Then another face appeared, and another. They started coming really fast. Some were young, some old. All different. I started feeling heavy and really bad inside. I turned the mirror face down. "Let's get this back to Hades."

Freddie nodded. Just as I jammed the mirror into his backpack, we heard a thumping sound. "What's that?" I whispered.

"I don't know," cried Freddie.

We stood back to back, looking out over the grass. The thumping got louder and louder. Then, crashing through the side hedge, came a monster! Half man, half bull, with really long, sharp horns sticking out of its forehead.

Freddie and I froze.

Just at that moment the cell phone rang.

I couldn't move. My eyes were glued to the monster as he snorted and grunted. The phone kept ringing. Finally, I pulled it out, flipped open the cover and held it to my ear.

"What do you mean, you love me?"

"Rosalie?"

"You can't just say something like that and then hang up."

"Rosalie!" I screamed. "Is your computer still on?"

"Yes, but —"

"Does it say anything about a monster in the labyrinth?!"

"A *what*?"

"A *monster*! Some kind of animal or something? Please look! Please! Right now!"

"All right! All right! Give me a minute."

The monster started snuffling toward us. "Hurry!" I shouted.

Freddie and I jumped off the stone and ran to where I'd dropped the thread — our only way out.

The monster lunged at us.

We screamed and took off in different

directions. That confused it for a second, trying to keep its eyes on both of us at the same time.

"The minotaur," Rosalie's voice came through the phone. I held it to my ear.

"The what?"

"The *minotaur*. That's the only animal mentioned. Well, it isn't exactly an animal — it says it's half human, half bull with —"

"Long horns sticking out of its forehead?"

"How did you know?"

The Minotaur came rushing at me. "Because I'm looking at it!" I yelled, then circled back around the podium. When it came around on my right, I went left. When it went left, I went right. It was getting madder by the minute, snorting loudly. Smoke shot out of its nose.

I put the phone to my ear again. "Rosalie! Does it say anything about how to get away from it?"

"Not on this site."

"Well, try another one!"

The Minotaur and I kept going around the podium. "Freddie! Help!"

Freddie was standing by the exit with the thread clenched in his fist. "What can I do?!" He was bawling again.

"Alex? Are you there?"

"Yes! Yes! Did you find something?"

"It was once subdued by music. It lulled the Minotaur to sleep!"

"Music?"

"That's all it says."

"Okay! Thanks!"

I jammed the phone into my jacket pocket. "Freddie?"

"Yeah?"

"Stop crying and sing."

"What?"

"The Minotaur gets lulled to sleep with music."

"How do *you* know?"

"Just start singing."

"*Singing?*"

"You heard me. Sing! Sing a lullaby! Something lulling."

"Are you nuts?"

"Sing, Freddie!!"

"Rock-a-bye baby, on the tree top ..."

"Slower!"

"When the wind blows, the cradle will rock ..."

"Louder!"

"When the bough breaks, the cradle will fall." Freddie's voice was shaking but he didn't sound half bad. "And down will come baby, cradle and all."

The Minotaur finally heard him and stopped snorting. It slowly turned its head toward Freddie.

Freddie stopped singing. The Minotaur snorted again.

"Keep singing!" I yelled.

"From the high rooftops, down to the sea ..."

I joined in. "No one's as dear, as baby to me."

The Minotaur got sleepier and sleepier.

"Wee little fingers, eyes wide and bright ..."

It lowered its body to the ground.

"Now sound asleep ..."

Its eyes closed and it went over on its side.

"Until morning light."

I kept humming as I tiptoed past its huge head and around the sharp horns. When I reached Freddie, we quietly followed the thread back through the labyrinth.

When we stepped out the main entrance, we were instantly hit with that blast of light again. The next thing we knew, we were back in the palace with Hades and Tiresias.

20

"Ah, I see you did not return with the mirror," said Hades. "How unfortunate."

"It's right here," I said, unzipping Freddie's backpack. When I handed it over, he looked really surprised. A couple of seconds later he said, "I will have to forego the pleasure of your company, Tiresias."

"It appears so," said Tiresias. "Now, I'm afraid we must depart. Tartarus awaits."

Hades looked at Freddie and me and, in a kind voice, said, "You must be tired after your journey."

Freddie nodded. "You're not kidding."

"Then rest awhile and enjoy some refreshment." He waved his arm. A mist swirled around and when it disappeared we saw a large table covered with food. "A little something to celebrate your success."

"No thank you," I said. "We ate a huge meal just before we got here."

"What huge meal?" asked Freddie.

I tried to give him a don't-you-dare-touch-any-food look, but he didn't get it. "Remember the fries?" I said. "And those apple turnovers? You ordered *two* of them."

Freddie frowned, but when he saw me nodding toward Tiresias, he finally clued in.

"Oh yeah, humongous. How could I forget?" He turned to Hades. "I really couldn't eat another bite. Thanks anyway."

"A little honey cake, perhaps?"

"Sorry," I said. "I'm allergic to sugar. Break out in hives big as anthills."

Hades looked disappointed. "Perhaps on your next visit."

"Sure. Thanks."

"Can't wait," added Freddie.

Hades tucked the mirror under his arm and said, "Follow me."

As we passed the table, Freddie grabbed something. I slapped it out of his hand.

"It was one measly olive, for crying out loud!"

Freddie and I veered toward the gold door.

"That is not the passage to Tartarus," said Hades.

"But, the *dungeon* door leads to the labyrinth," I said.

Hades smirked. "They both lead to the labyrinth." And then he laughed.

"Very funny," said Freddie sarcastically.

Hades spun around. "You dare to mock me?"

Freddie froze, then made some squeaking sounds. I glared at him. He mouthed, "I'm sorry."

Hades turned away and led us down dim hallways out into a yard covered in what looked like ash. Then he went over to a stone hut and opened the door. "This is the passage to Tartarus," he said and waved us in.

Inside the hut we saw a winding stone staircase built into the ground. It looked like it went down forever. When we looked up, Hades was gone.

"Come," said Tiresias, and started down the staircase.

After going around and around for ages, Freddie and I felt like we were going to throw up. But that wasn't nearly as bad as the heavy feeling that came over us — like when I looked into the mirror, only much, much worse.

The lower we went, the sicker we became, and the slower we moved. "I've never felt this bad in my whole life."

"It is our proximity to Tartarus," said Tiresias. "There is so much sadness and suffering that the very air is filled with it."

A little while later, Tiresias stopped.

"What's wrong?" I asked.

"Before we go any farther, there is one condition I must insist upon."

"Don't eat anything," said Freddie, flopping down on the step and leaning his head against the wall.

"That is not the condition."

"Whatever it is, we'll do it," I said.

"When we get to Tartarus, you may see things that disturb you. However, you are not permitted, under *any* circumstances, to interfere — in any manner. We are here to help right the wrong committed by one soul, and one soul only."

"We understand," I said.

Freddie nodded.

"You must *promise* to obey me in this," insisted Tiresias.

Freddie and I both promised.

"Then we may proceed."

We went down the last hundred or so steps. The lower we got, the darker it became. The last step was an open space. Up ahead stood a row of burned, shriveled-up trees, like after a forest fire.

"Is this Tartarus?" asked Freddie weakly.

"Not yet," said Tiresias.

On the other side of the trees was a steep hill, made of charcoal. We had to go up sideways, holding on to each other so we wouldn't slide back down. When we reached the top, we were standing in front of a high black fence, stretching as far as our eyes could see.

"We have arrived," said Tiresias. "Prepare yourselves."

Hissing sounds came from above. In a tower sat a woman dressed in a dark purple robe. Snakes slithered around her arms and waist. They hissed and darted their tongues out.

"Welcome to Tartarus," said the woman.

The ground suddenly shifted under our feet.

"What's happening?!" cried Freddie.

Roots sprang up, wound tightly around our ankles — and pulled us down into the earth.

21

My worst nightmare is being buried alive. And now it was happening! Wake up! Wake up! I screamed inside my head. But I didn't wake up.

Just when I thought my lungs would burst, the earth spit us out.

We lay on the ground gasping, covered in dirt and slime. Tiresias helped Freddie and me up and walked us over to a large pond surrounded by pointy rocks. We waded in.

The water felt go good I swam around, washing the dirt off my face and body and out of my hair. When I surfaced, Freddie's eyes were almost popping out of his head. I thought he was staring at me, then I realized he was staring *behind* me. I whirled around. A head was floating on the water. I screamed and swam away as fast as I could.

It was a man's head, with really dry skin and cracked, swollen lips. "Please, help me," it said.

"He's alive!" Freddie shouted and dashed behind Tiresias.

"My thirst is great." The voice was barely above a whisper. "My mouth is parched."

"Drink the water!" I yelled.

He lowered his lips but the water moved away. He looked up at me. "I cannot." He sounded so weak and tired. "You must help me."

"Come out!" shouted Freddie. "Maybe you can drink from the shore!"

"I am buried. I cannot move."

"Buried?" I turned to Tiresias. "How can he be buried in water?"

"It is his fate," said Tiresias.

"His *fate*?"

"We must go now."

"We've got to help him! He's dying of thirst!"

"He is already dead."

"Please help me," begged the man.

I couldn't stand it. I stepped back into the water when I heard, "Remember your promise."

That stopped me cold. Freddie and I had both promised not to interfere in any way, no matter what we saw. But ... the man's eyes were so sad!

"I beg you," he said.

I'd never broken a promise, but I couldn't just walk away. I don't know why but I suddenly thought of my dad. What if it was him begging for help and people just let him suffer? My heart hurt so bad I almost cried.

In a really gentle voice, Freddie said, "Let's go."

I slowly turned and started walking away.

"*Please.*" The man's voice was almost a moan.

Keep walking, I told myself. Just keep walking.

But I couldn't. I swung around, ran back and dove into the water.

"Alex! Don't!"

I swam over to the man, cupped my hands and filled them with water. I held them up to his lips, and he drank. But no matter how much water I gave him, he was still thirsty. There was nothing I could do.

"You have a kind heart," said Tiresias when we'd started walking again. "Unfortunately, there will be consequences."

As we continued, I realized that I couldn't hear the sound of our footsteps. And Freddie's lips were moving but I couldn't hear what he was saying. "What's going on?" I asked. No sound came out.

A gust of wind swept ash into the air and made it dance in circles. I heard a door bang. How could there be a door? We were outside.

Freddie and Tiresias just kept walking and talking like everything was normal. But it wasn't. My heart started pounding. The dust got so thick I had to squint to keep it out of my eyes. When it finally cleared, I was all alone, standing in a long hallway with a door at the far end. It looked like the walls were made of the shriveled trees.

Suddenly, I heard a sound coming from behind the door. I walked over to it, reached out and turned the knob. My hands shook as I pushed the door open.

The room had one window and was completely empty except for some leaves swirling around the floor. Only there wasn't any wind. What was blowing them? Stepping inside, I felt cobwebs brush against my face. The minute I broke the threads, the window burst open and waves of dust poured in, covering me. I shut my eyes but the dust seeped right through the lids. It went into my mouth too. I felt like I was drying up. Then a voice said, "Thou art dust and unto dust thou shalt return."

I'd heard those words before — at funerals! Just before they buried somebody!

I opened my mouth to scream and when I did, dust flew up my nose. I sneezed really loudly.

When I opened my eyes, I was back on the path with Freddie and Tiresias.

"Where'd you go?" shouted Freddie. Then he saw my face. "You look just like that head in the water!"

"Consequences," said Tiresias, and kept walking.

I couldn't believe he was going to leave me like this. So much dust was stuck to my face that no matter how hard I tried, I couldn't wipe it all off.

"Wait a sec," Freddie said. Then he pulled off his backpack and unzipped it. He yanked out some baseball cards, a comic book and that bag of green grapes. I would have given anything to be able to get some of their juice into my mouth, but maybe Tartarus was like Hades — if you ate anything, you were staying for good. "It's here somewhere," said Freddie, digging deeper.

I tried to speak but my mouth was too dry. Finally, Freddie pulled out a little bag holding a plastic fork, a knife and a wet wipe. "I saved this from my last takeout." He ripped open the bag, tore the foil around the wet wipe, then gently rubbed it against my lips and eyes. It felt great.

"You saved my life, Freddie."

"Hey, what are friends for?"

We caught up to Tiresias. "Look there," he said, pointing at a small hill. We saw a red light flicker in the distance. As we stared at it, a black triangle came over the crest and moved quickly toward us.

Freddie began to shake. "What's *that*?"

"The Chamber of Darkness," said Tiresias.

The triangle grew bigger and bigger, surrounding us until there was nothing but blackness. It was like we were inside a tomb.

"I can't stand not being able to see!" cried Freddie.

"Keep your wits about you," said Tiresias firmly.

Maybe we couldn't see anything, but we could hear, and what we heard made our skin crawl. Voices were crying and shrieking and wailing. It was *horrible*.

"Where'd they come from?" I yelled.

"They are not here," said Tiresias.

"Yes they are!"

The voices cried out, "Mercy! Have mercy!"

Freddie started to whimper, then he shouted, "I gotta get outta here!"

"Stand your ground!" ordered Tiresias. "Remember your purpose."

The pitch black terrified us.

"I'm gonna die, Alex." Freddie grabbed on to me. "I'm gonna die."

I knew how he felt. The shrieking and crying was so terrible it was sucking the life right out of us. The darkness made it even more unbearable.

If only we could see. That's when I remembered the flashlight I'd taken to Slug's house. I pulled it out of my pocket and flicked it on.

Amazing! It still worked. The instant the light came on, all the sounds stopped.

"Oh, Alex, thank you! Thank you!"

I quickly flashed the beam around. No one was there. All we saw were the shriveled trees.

"Where'd everybody go?" I asked.

"The silence is so deep here, sound travels far," said Tiresias.

"Then where are they?"

"In the Well of Souls."

"And just where would that be?" asked Freddie.

"Stay on the path," said Tiresias. "We will arrive soon."

We stuck close together, the circle of light leading our way. As we moved along, it got colder and colder. I kept my eyes open for something that looked like a well. "Are the souls in a real well?"

"It is underground like a well, but it is a chamber where those who have committed murder are kept in containment."

The path suddenly got really slippery — Freddie and I fell down hard. Only we didn't land on ground. It was ice. The flashlight flew out of my hand and slid away. I scrambled over to get it. When I reached to pick it up, I yelled and fell back. Faces were looking at me from under the ice!

Freddie crawled over. "What's wrong?" Then he saw the faces. The souls pressed their hands against the ice, their eyes desperate and their mouths saying words we couldn't hear. But we knew what they wanted — to get out.

"Tiresias!" Freddie and I shouted.

As Tiresias made his way over, I spotted Costas.

"Turn off the light," Tiresias ordered.

"No!" cried Freddie.

"Just for a moment."

I flicked off the light and everything went black.

"This is the first light these souls have seen in a very, very long time," explained Tiresias. "They are drawn to it like moths to a flame."

"Poor things," said Freddie.

"Feel no sorrow. There is *great* evil here."

"Not Costas!" I said.

"Not all. You are correct."

"Can we turn the light on now?" asked Freddie. "I'm getting creeped out."

The ice under me felt funny, like it was moving. Just as I opened my mouth to tell Tiresias, something tugged at my legs. Freddie must have felt the same thing because we both screamed. Suddenly, we were yanked up off the ice. Our bodies flew through the air and we landed on solid ground. What was happening? I flicked on the flashlight. Tiresias was standing over us.

"I am sorry if I hurt you," he said.

"What'd ya do that for?" cried Freddie.

"Your body heat was melting the ice. Human energy is very powerful, especially in this place."

I shook my head. "This is unbelievable."

"Do not underestimate the warmth of a living soul. It radiates in ways you will never understand." He helped us up. "These souls will stop at nothing to get light and heat. The heat from your body."

"Well, I don't have any to spare," said Freddie, rubbing his arms. "It's *freezing*."

I told Tiresias that I'd seen Costas under the ice.

"How are we ever going to get him out?" Freddie asked.

"By melting the spot where he is," I said.

"Are you nuts? They'll *all* escape!"

"This evil must *not* be allowed to spread through the Underworld," said Tiresias.

Freddie shook his head. "So, Alex, just how do you plan to let *one* escape without the rest of them tagging along?"

"We'll psych them out," I said. "Like a football play. The souls go wherever the light is, right?" I turned to Freddie. "You distract them with the flashlight. I'll get Costas out."

"But won't he follow the light, *too*?"

"Leave that to me," said Tiresias.

We made our way back toward the well. After about twenty steps, I felt the ground turn slippery. The souls looked up and pressed their faces against the ice, clawing at it. Freddie kept moving to the far side of the well.

"That's Costas," I said to Tiresias, pointing to one of the faces.

Tiresias looked directly at him. *I have a message for you.* He didn't say it out loud but I heard him.

The other souls ignored Tiresias and kept grabbing for the light.

"Are you ready?" I shouted to Freddie.

"Ready!"

I threw the flashlight up in an arc and then Freddie caught it. He aimed the beam straight down. Within a second, the souls had shot over to him. "They're here!"

I dropped to my knees and pressed my hands against the ice. I could feel it melting. Costas's spirit slid through.

I yanked my hands away.

"He's out!" I shouted to Freddie. "Get off the ice!"

Freddie ran, but he slipped and fell. "Oh nooo!"

His body had melted the ice. Souls poured through the opening and scattered in every direction.

"What are we gonna do?" screamed Freddie, dashing over to us.

We heard loud hissing sounds.

Then we saw them.

Huge snakes, hundreds of them, surrounded the souls. Tiresias said, "Hold on to my robe." We didn't ask why, just grabbed. Tiresias stepped into the air and disappeared.

I don't know how, but we could see everything. The woman who guarded the gates of Tartarus suddenly appeared. She watched as the snakes drove the souls, wailing and shrieking, back into the well. Then she blew on the ice and it froze over again.

"Costas, she will soon realize you are missing," said Tiresias. "We must move quickly."

22

We kept a good hold on Tiresias's robe as he moved, and instantly we found ourselves inside a crack in the wall of a mountain.

This didn't look right. "Where are we?"

"I miscalculated," said Tiresias. "I apologize."

Freddie looked worried. "*Miscalculated?*"

"We are not far from the cliff."

"*What* cliff?"

I could see light at the end of the crevice, but it sure didn't look very close. Costas just walked on ahead, toward the light, but the rest of us had to move sideways through the narrow space. We slid our feet along, pressing our hands against the rock face. At some points it got so tight I didn't think we'd make it through.

"I can't breathe," cried Freddie.

"Take off your backpack."

He tried, but there wasn't enough room for his arms to slip it off. "I can't!"

"This is the narrowest part," I said. "A bit farther up it gets wider. I can see it."

Pretty soon there was enough room to walk

facing forward. We moved along quickly, keeping our eyes on the opening. "Almost there," I said.

Just then we heard a loud rumbling.

"That can't be good," whispered Freddie.

It wasn't. Rocks were falling. Then the mountain groaned and the sides started closing in.

"It's gonna crush us!" screamed Freddie. "We're gonna die!"

"Run!" shouted Costas from the opening.

We ran toward him. I cleared the mountain and yelled to the others. "Come on!"

A rock slammed hard against Freddie's knee. He yelled and went down.

Tiresias went back for him as the sides of the mountain pressed in closer and closer. Tiresias lifted Freddie and was helping him along, but there was no way they were going to make it. "Throw me your backpack!" I yelled.

Freddie whipped it off and Tiresias threw it to me. I yanked out the crowbar and held it between the moving walls of rock. They pushed against the ends and stopped. But the sound didn't.

"Hurry!"

Tiresias practically carried Freddie the rest of the way. I could see the pressure building against the crowbar. It was starting to bend.

"Hurry!"

Just as Tiresias and Freddie squeezed through the opening, the crowbar snapped and the mountain closed.

Freddie fell to the ground, crying in pain. His leg stuck straight out to the side. Broken for sure.

"He needs a doctor!" I shouted.

"The Sacred River in my village," said Costas. "Its water has great healing power."

"Tiresias!" I called, but he just walked away. "Tiresias!"

I ran and caught up with him at the edge of the cliff. "We've got to do something to help Freddie. Costas says —"

"The portal to Greece in Costas's time is at the base of this cliff."

I looked over the edge. Huge waves crashed against the rocks below.

"And how do we get there?"

"We jump."

"*Jump*?" Was he crazy?

"The portal will open. Trust me."

Tiresias suddenly closed his eyes and listened. Everything was silent. He quickly walked back to Freddie. "We must hurry. They're coming."

As he helped him up, Freddie screamed in pain.

"What are you *doing*?!" I yelled.

"We must get him to the portal," said Tiresias. "Now!"

"He can't be moved!"

"We have no choice."

"What? You're going to throw him over the cliff?!"

"Yes."

"I won't let you do that!"

"If we remain here, his suffering will be much greater. As will ours."

"Then heal him!"

"There is no *time*!"

I saw a look in Tiresias's eyes I hadn't seen before. He was scared. I wrapped Freddie's arm around my shoulder and grabbed him around the waist. Tiresias did the same on the other side. Together we dragged him toward the edge of the cliff.

I glared at Costas. "Why did you tell me about the river if we can't get to it? Why would you *do* that?"

"There are ways."

Tiresias got really angry. "*Costas! There is no time!*"

As we neared the edge, Freddie freaked. "Noooooo!" He let out a long, terrified wail and tried to wriggle out of our grasp. "He's trying to kill us, Alex!"

"He's gotten us this far," I said. "We *have* to trust him."

Freddie yanked away and fell to the ground. He was way too scared to believe what I was saying. I'm not sure I believed it either.

Tiresias leaned down. Freddie kicked out with his good leg and screamed, "Get away from me! Get away!"

Tiresias looked really mad. "Foolish *mortal*." He spat out the words then turned and disappeared.

I whirled around. "Where'd he go?"

Before Costas could answer, we heard screeching, like the sound of scared monkeys.

"They're here," said Costas.

The screeching got even louder. Then, up over the lip of the cliff rose three creatures. Their bodies looked human but their heads were small and ugly, with black eyes and sharp teeth. They had claws for hands, and their feet were hooves. Huge bat wings sprang from their shoulders.

Suddenly, Tiresias reappeared holding a small clay bowl. When he saw the creatures, he shouted, "Alex! Run!"

As I took off back toward the mountain, I saw one of the creatures hover right in front of Costas. Neither of them moved.

I didn't look where I was going — just wanted

to get away. Tripping over the backpack, I landed on my stomach. The second creature flew up behind me and plunged its claws into my shoulder. I screamed in pain but twisted around and kicked at it. It flew off.

Tiresias was bending over Freddie, protecting him from the third creature. He poured water on Freddie's leg.

The creature that had come after me now attacked Tiresias. It plunged its sharp teeth into his face, ripping off the flesh. I picked up a rock and threw it, hard. It hit the creature's head, sending it flying over the cliff. It plunged straight down.

The other creature flew back at me, snapping its teeth.

"Cover your eyes!" shouted Tiresias.

I slammed my hands over my eyes as the great bat wings beat against my body. Claws dug into me and my hands were wrenched away. As sharp teeth snapped at my eyes, I saw Freddie running at the creature, yanking him off me by its wings.

It turned on him.

I grabbed the backpack, threw in some heavy rocks and zipped it up. Spinning the backpack around my head, I whipped it across the creature's back, then across its head, sending it hurling sideways.

"The cliff!" shouted Tiresias. "RUN!"

The creature guarding Costas heard him and flew straight at Tiresias.

Tiresias barely got his arms up before the creature was on him, ripping his flesh.

"Leave him alone!" I screamed, running toward them. I flung the backpack as hard as I could, catching the creature in the back of the head. Screeching, it dropped Tiresias and lay still.

I was crying and shaking like crazy as I knelt beside Tiresias. Lifting his shoulders, I rested his head on my knees. "It's all my *fault*."

"Do not weep for me," he whispered. "Death is a blessing."

"Please don't die!"

"I shall return to the Elysian Fields no longer weighed down by the limitations of mortal flesh … You have set me free."

"It is because of me that you die," Costas whispered.

Tiresias smiled. "It is because of you … that I live."

His eyes closed and his body went limp. I held him, rocking back and forth.

"Alex!"

My head snapped up. Three more creatures had appeared.

I yelled, "The cliff!"

Freddie let a rock fly, hitting one of the creatures in the chest. Then he raced toward the cliff.
As the creatures flew at us, I lowered Tiresias's
head to the ground and ran.

Freddie and I leaped off the cliff.

23

Everything turned white and then bright lights flashed. Suddenly I was treading water in a cool lake. The setting sun filled the sky with beautiful pink and orange clouds. Freddie was waving at me from the shore. "How'd you get there?" I shouted.

He shrugged. "Beats me."

"Where's Costas?"

A puff of smoke moved over the water's surface and, as it reached Freddie, turned into a man.

Costas was human again.

I swam to shore. Costas was about eighteen years old, with golden skin and long, curly black hair. He looked so happy he almost glowed. "I am home again. How is it *possible* that we are here?"

"Tiresias," I said.

Costas's face turned serious. "The Eternal Flame."

I nodded. "You have a chance to make things right."

"But I know not where the flame is hidden."

"We'll help you find it."

"What day is it? We must find out." He started walking so fast that Freddie and I had a hard time keeping up. After about ten minutes, we were lagging behind.

"Where are you going, Costas?" Freddie called out.

But Costas just kept moving. About five minutes later we heard horses' hooves clattering on dry ground. Costas ran back and pushed us behind some bushes. Seven riders rode by. They were all wearing deep-blue cloaks that fluttered behind them.

"Who are they?" asked Freddie.

"Members of the secret society," said Costas.

I looked at him. "But you were blindfolded."

"My friend is among them."

"That's some friend."

"He has suffered greatly for his actions."

"How do you know?" I asked.

"I met his soul in Tartarus. He begged my forgiveness."

"Did you forgive him?" asked Freddie.

Costas looked at him. "Those who most need forgiving must forgive."

Freddie looked confused, but I think I understood what he meant.

"They seemed to be in a real hurry," I said.

"When they travel in a group like that, it is always to a meeting."

"Where?"

He shrugged.

We started off after the horses. Soon the sun set and it was pretty dark.

About half an hour later, we heard the sound of babies crying.

"What are babies doing way out here?" Freddie asked.

"They are not babies," said Costas. "They are pigs."

"*Pigs?*"

"The screams of pigs most closely resemble the human cry."

The crying turned to shrieks.

"Someone's hurting them!" I hissed.

"Not yet," said Costas, "but they sense impending death."

"Is some farmer gonna kill them?" Freddie asked.

Costas shook his head. "It is a ritual slaughter." This didn't sound good. "These ceremonies always take place near the sea."

He led us behind some boulders overlooking a beach. The golden flames of a torch danced in the darkness. Chanting mixed with the pigs' cries.

Someone lifted the torch and the flame moved through the darkness. It lit a second torch and that one lit a third and so on, until seven were burning. The light from the flames lit up the whole area. Each torch was held by a member of the secret society, standing in a circle around a large crate of squirming pigs.

One of the members walked away from the circle and touched his flame to the ground. An area about the size of a grave instantly turned red, as if it was covered with burning coals.

"What're they doing?" I whispered to Costas.

"Pigs are often sacrificed as a funeral custom."

"Funeral?"

"It cleanses a family of the taint of death."

I didn't get it, but before I could ask the chanting stopped.

Somebody was walking toward the group. As he entered the circle, the members of the secret society knelt down.

The man, wearing a dark-red cloak, had long black hair and a short beard. His dark eyes looked around at each face. As he turned our way, Costas gasped.

"Who is it?" I whispered.

"Prince Dameon, brother of King Talasius."

The prince raised his sword and in a loud

voice said, "Death is the beginning of birth."

"Is he gonna kill the pigs?" Freddie sounded really upset.

Costas didn't answer, just looked confused. "*He* is the leader of the society?"

I nodded. "And he becomes king, too."

"*Talasius* is king."

"Not for much longer. Tiresias told us that after his baby dies, King Talasius goes crazy. Then his brother takes over."

The look in Costas's eyes changed. "Now I understand."

The prince was speaking again. "Death leads to the birth of that which is nobler."

The guy to the right of the prince held a box. "What d'ya think's in the box?" asked Freddie.

The prince walked around the circle and stopped in front of one of the members.

"That is my friend, Porteus," whispered Costas.

The prince lowered his sword onto Porteus's shoulder. The guy holding the box walked over to them and opened the lid. Porteus lifted out a sack tied with a cord. Then he bowed deeply, turned and walked away along the beach.

A member of the society opened the crate and grabbed one of the little pigs. The chanting started again. The pig squealed and wriggled,

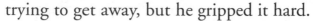

trying to get away, but he gripped it hard.

The prince led the way down to the water. Everyone followed. Chanting mixed with squealing. It made my skin crawl.

I turned to Costas. "We have to do something!"

"Be still!"

The pig was held in the air for a second then pushed under the water. Suddenly, I found myself darting across the beach.

"Alex!!"

I lifted the crate lid, grabbed the bars and tipped it over. While the pigs squealed loudly and ran off in different directions, I raced back to the boulder.

The boy holding the pig underwater loosened his grip. The pig scrambled to shore and took off, too. The chase was on.

"Way to go, Alex!" said Freddie, smiling.

Costas looked really mad. "Your action was foolish! If we are caught, we will be *killed*!"

"But I couldn't just ..."

"Silence!"

"We're wasting time," I said.

"We are safe here."

"Costas, if you want to save your soul, you're going to have to save that baby first."

He stared at me. "You are right." His voice was

gentler now. "Yet this mortal body is filled with fear."

"We're scared, too!"

Freddie nodded. "Big time."

Costas gave us a little smile. "The palace is not far."

What with the darkness and all the commotion, no one saw us make our way toward the horses.

Costas heaved me up on one and Freddie on another. He untied all the others, leaped onto a horse, dug his heels into its sides and galloped away.

Our horses followed. The others took off.

24

Costas was right, the palace wasn't far. Good thing too, because Freddie and I bounced like crazy the whole way.

We dismounted near the grounds. "The palace is just through the olive grove." Costas pointed to his right. "We must walk from here. And quietly."

Costas led us through the grove, then across a field. In the silence we heard a horse whinny. We turned in that direction, pushing through thick brambles. Soon we spotted Porteus sitting on his horse staring at the palace. He didn't move a muscle. Just stared.

There were small windows about halfway up the palace wall, but nothing big enough to crawl through. And the walls were flat — no arches, no balconies — nothing.

"What's he waiting for?" asked Freddie.

Costas looked at the windows, then at Porteus, then back again. "Perhaps for a signal."

"What kind of signal? And from who?" I asked.

"I do not know."

We waited but nothing happened. Porteus kept staring at the windows.

I was getting bored. "We can't just hang around watching. We have to get inside."

Costas nodded and quietly led the way to the front of the palace. It was huge, with three large bronze domes that shone in the moonlight. Gold and blue banners hung under every window, and guards stood at the arched gates. They wore dark tunics and silver helmets and they carried spears.

"Should we ask if we can talk to the king?" said Freddie.

"No," answered Costas.

"We *have* to warn him about what's going to happen!" I said.

"If we warn him, he will know that we were part of the plan. The Eternal Flame has been stolen and his son has not yet been named. He will not be welcoming."

Freddie frowned. "What's the big deal? Can't he just give him a name?"

"Even a king cannot change this law. It is decreed by the gods."

"What's the worst that can happen if the baby

doesn't get named?"

I looked at Freddie. "Don't you remember what Tiresias said? The soul of an unnamed child roams the earth forever."

"Oh yeah."

"Without a name," said Costas, "you do not belong. You are a lost soul."

I remembered Dad saying that that's what they called people who were buried without a coin in their mouth. Lost souls. Costas and that baby had a lot in common.

We were startled by a loud crackling sound coming from the ground near us. Suddenly the leaves moved! As we backed away, we heard a grunt. A little pig popped up through the leaves.

"Hey, Piggy!" Freddie scooped him into his arms. "How'd you get here all by yourself?"

"Release him," said Costas. "We have more important matters to attend to."

Freddie scratched the piglet's head but didn't let him go.

I looked back at the gates. "How do we get in?"

Costas scanned the area. "I know of no other way in except past the guards."

"Then we need a diversion."

"Like what?" asked Freddie.

The pig nuzzled Freddie's cheek.

"Like him," I said. "*He's* our diversion."

"My buddy here?"

"Costas, take off your belt and tunic."

Freddie looked surprised as Costas handed them over. I wrapped the tunic around the pig and tied the belt twice around his body. "The belt's way too big," said Freddie.

"That's okay." I grabbed some branches and tucked them into the belt. The poor little pig had no idea what was going on.

When we were sure the branches wouldn't fall out, we made our way over to the palace wall and quietly moved as close to the gates as we could without being seen. At the last second I pulled the tunic over the pig's head, put him down and gave him a hard push toward the guards. The belt clasp scraped along the stones, and the branches flapped up and down. The guards looked stunned for a second and then took off after it.

Costas, Freddie and I slipped through the gates.

Inside we found ourselves in a big courtyard with statues and a huge pool of water. Around it were marble columns with paintings of animals.

"Bed chambers are on the second level," Costas said, heading for a winding staircase. We climbed up and then went along two empty corridors past lots of closed doors. "Which one's the nursery?" I whispered.

"There," he said, pointing at a door with a garland of flowers above it.

We crept to the door and listened. No sound came from inside. "Are babies guarded?" asked Freddie.

"Only by their nurse," said Costas. "She may be there."

"I'll knock on the door," I said. "If she answers, we grab her."

Freddie nodded. So did Costas.

I slowly reached out and knocked softly. No answer. "Maybe she didn't hear," whispered Freddie. "Knock a little harder."

"I don't want to wake the baby."

"Then we must go in," said Costas.

I slowly turned the handle and quietly pushed the door open. Then I stuck my head in and looked around. "No one's here." We slipped inside and closed the door behind us.

There was a small oil lamp, a water jug and a vase of flowers on a stand by the door. We could see the baby's cradle and beautiful tapestries on the walls. Behind the cradle were two curtains. The baby was sleeping peacefully under a white blanket.

Costas crept over to the shuttered window. "This is the only way in. But how will Porteus climb the wall?"

We heard footsteps coming down the corridor. "Hide!"

We looked around for a closet or something but there wasn't one.

"Where?" cried Freddie.

"The curtain!" said Costas, and he pushed us behind it just as the door opened. We couldn't see who came in and were way too scared to look.

"Sleep peacefully, sweet prince." It was a woman's voice.

I thought it might be the queen, but the voice sounded hard. There was no love in it. Whoever it was walked over to the window — we heard the shutters open. I peeked around the edge of the curtain and saw a large woman with a shawl over her head holding the oil lamp. Must be the nurse, I thought. She held the lamp outside the window, moving it slowly to the left, then to the right. She was definitely signaling.

Porteus!

She returned to the baby and pulled out a long rope. Tying one end to the base of the cradle, she walked to the window, unwinding it.

Then she flung the rest of the rope down the side of the palace.

It didn't make sense. Porteus would be way too heavy to climb a rope tied to a cradle.

Just then the baby started crying.

The nurse must have come back because we heard her muttering to the baby.

"Be still, little prince."

As soon as he stopped crying, she quickly moved to the window. We saw her pull a jar out of her pocket. Removing the top, she leaned out the window and carefully poured a thin stream of white liquid down the length of rope. Then she sprinkled the liquid along the rope between the window and the cradle. When she got to the cradle, she yanked the blanket off the baby — just like we saw in the mirror of Costas's deeds. Then she sprinkled more liquid on the baby's legs and tucked the jar into her pocket.

"It's almost time, little prince," she whispered. Keeping her eyes glued to the window, she started humming.

Everything was quiet except for the sound of the baby cooing. Costas's eyes darted from the window to the cradle and back again.

The nurse moved to the door and stood absolutely still, watching the window. What was going on? My heart pounded so hard I thought somebody would hear.

We saw the head first. Its tongue flicked in and out.

Then another head!

Then a body crawled up over the window ledge — a gray two-headed snake, about the length of my arm.

It coiled around and around the rope, lapping up the liquid, slithering toward the cradle.

Costas stood frozen. I grabbed his arm and shook him — he had to stop the snake from killing the baby or everything we'd done would be for nothing! His soul would go back to the Chamber of Darkness for all eternity.

The snake got closer and closer to the cradle.

I shook Costas again but still he didn't move. Beads of sweat appeared on his forehead.

He was terrified.

The snake continued moving slowly toward the cradle. When it slithered inside, Freddie gasped.

The nurse must have heard him because suddenly the curtain was yanked open.

The nurse was a man!

He reached out, grabbed Freddie and flung him to the floor, hard. Costas stayed hidden in the shadows.

I raced toward the cradle but before I could reach it, something slammed into my back, pitching me forward. Then I felt myself being lifted right off the floor and jammed against the door. The man wrapped his fingers tightly around my neck and held me there.

My eyes darted to the baby. The snake was on the blanket!

I tried to kick out, but the man only tightened his grip. He turned to watch.

A drop of white liquid rolled down the baby's little leg just as the snake reached it. Its fanged and gaping mouths opened wide, ready to strike.

"Noooo!!"

The curtain got wrenched right out of the ceiling as Costas lurched forward and grabbed the snake with both hands. He held it away from him, but the snake's fangs pierced his hand over and over. He yelled in pain as he raced to the window and flung the snake into the night.

The next thing I knew, Freddie was up. The water jug cracked against the man's skull and he slumped to the floor. So did I.

Costas was on his knees, gripping his hand. "Is the prince safe?"

We looked over. The baby was kicking and gurgling.

"He's fine." I knelt beside Costas. "You saved his life."

Costas nodded. "Good."

"We have to get you to a doctor," said Freddie.

Costas shook his head. "It is my destiny to die."

"We've got to try!" I said through gritted teeth.

"Precious time will be wasted. You must find the Eternal Flame and return it to the Sacred Hearth in the square. What good will it have done to save the child if he still cannot be named? And other children will follow. They must not suffer this fate."

"But where are we going to find the flame?"

Costas nodded toward the man slumped by the door. "He will know."

Freddie and I helped Costas lie down. His body shivered. We dragged the curtain across the floor and tucked it in around him. His eyes were half closed and his breathing shallow. The swelling on his hand got bigger.

I looked deep into his eyes. "You are a hero, Costas." My voice caught in my throat. "The Elysian Fields will be your home now."

Costas smiled weakly, then shook his head again. "As before ... I am unable to pay."

I'd completely forgotten about Charon. "He's going to be stuck at the river again!"

"No he won't," said Freddie. He reached deep into his pocket and pulled out a gold coin.

"I thought you threw them all to Charon!"

"I kept one, for myself. But … it's for him."

I rested Costas's head on my knees, as I had done with Tiresias. "Everything's going to be okay. Here's your coin."

His eyes lit up and he smiled the most beautiful smile. Tears streamed down his face. "Thank you … for all you have done for me."

I had to blink hard to keep from crying.

Then his eyes dimmed. I lowered his head gently to the floor. Freddie slipped the coin between Costas's lips and I whispered, "Safe journey home."

Suddenly, a white light escaped from his mouth. It swirled around and disappeared.

The coin was gone.

25

"If that guy comes to," said Freddie, "he'll beat the crap out of us long before he tells us where the flame is."

"I've got an idea."

We dragged the man over to the window, untied the rope from the cradle and used it to tie his hands together. Then we lifted his arms over his head and tied the rope off around the window shutters.

Freddie grabbed the flower vase and handed it to me. I threw the water in the man's face. He came to, coughing and hacking.

His eyes quickly darted over to the baby.

"He's alive," I said.

He looked really mad and squirmed around to get loose, but the rope was too tight.

"Tell us where the Eternal Flame is."

"I will tell you nothing." He spit the words out.

"I knew he wouldn't," said Freddie.

I reached into his pocket, pulled out the jar and smelled what was inside. "It's sweet. Milk? I didn't know snakes liked milk."

I poured some liquid over the man's hands and head.

"The snake is dead," he laughed.

"Is it?" I looked out over the window. "Are you sure?"

The man swallowed hard.

"Tell us where the flame is."

He didn't answer, just turned away.

I leaned out the window like he had done and poured milk along the dangling rope. It didn't reach the ground anymore but he didn't know that. "If the snake's still alive, it'll find its way back ... right up to you."

I placed the jar on the floor beside him. Then I turned to Freddie. "Come on."

Freddie and I headed to the door. As I reached for the handle, the man shouted, "Pull up the rope!" We turned around. He looked scared. "I will tell you."

Freddie ran back and pulled up the rope.

"Promise me you will not throw it back after I tell you."

"If you tell us the truth," I said.

The man closed his eyes for a long time. Finally, he said, "The Eternal Flame is in the crypt under the palace at the far end of the Hall of the Dead. It lights the sarcophagus of the king's father."

Freddie looked surprised. "All this time it's been right under the king's nose!"

The man nodded.

"Didn't anyone wonder why the flame never went out?" I asked.

"It is my duty to keep it lit. Mine alone."

Now it made sense.

"Are there guards outside the crypt?" asked Freddie.

"Of course."

"Is there any other way to get in?" I asked.

"Yes, but obstacles are in place to stop anyone from entering."

"What obstacles?"

"That I do not know. They were placed after I hid the flame."

"Where's this other way in?"

"In the dark it will be impossible to find."

"Tell me anyway."

"If it is discovered that I told, I will be killed!"

"If you don't, the snake will kill you."

Finally, in a low voice, he said, "Deep in the woods, behind the palace, there is a door in the ground. It is covered with earth and leaves. But I speak the truth when I say it is impossible to find."

"You found it."

The man looked at me surprised.

"When you carried in the torch, you must have gone through that underground door. Otherwise someone would have seen you."

"Good thinking, Alex," said Freddie.

"Tell me how to find it. Or I can throw this rope down. Your choice."

Freddie and I made our way back along the corridors and down the stairs to the courtyard. The main gates were just around the corner. "The guards are bound to be back by now," whispered Freddie. "How are we gonna get past them *this* time?"

There were three large statues at the far end of the pool. They'd be way too heavy to move. Closer to us was a small marble Cupid holding his bow and arrow.

The splash alerted the guards. Freddie's cries for help brought them running.

Hiding behind one of the columns, we saw them dash past us. Then we circled around and ran out the gates, heading for the woods. The man had said to look for a low stone wall, then take twenty steps from its center to a tree with a gnarly trunk. The bark would look like faces.

The flashlight gave us just enough light to see

where we were going. When we found the center of the wall, we paced off twenty steps. I flashed the beam around. All the tree trunks were straight.

"He lied," said Freddie.

There sure wasn't a gnarly trunk with faces on it, but then I had a thought. "Wait a sec. Twenty steps for us and twenty steps for *him* wouldn't be the same distance. Let's go a little farther."

We went another five steps. The light from the flashlight started fading. I hit it against the palm of my hand, and as the light brightened, I quickly flashed it around. We spotted a huge, bent-over tree. The trunk and branches were twisted and the bark had round bumps all along it that looked like faces ... babies' faces.

"That's it!" cried Freddie, running up to it.

Then he disappeared.

26

"Freddie!"

I headed to the tree.

"Don't come any closer, Alex!"

I stopped in my tracks. "Where are you?"

"In the mud. Down here!"

I flashed the light on the ground at the base of the tree. Freddie was hip deep in mud. "Help me outta here," he yelled.

I reached to grab his outstretched hand when, with a sudden jolt, he sank up to his chest.

"Something's pulling me, Alex!"

I pushed a broken tree branch toward Freddie. "Grab hold. I'll pull you out!"

Freddie gripped the branch with both hands and held on tight. I pulled as hard as I could — but he wasn't moving. "Push off with your feet!" I shouted.

"I'm trying! But my legs won't move. The mud's too thick!"

I pulled again, using every ounce of my strength. Freddie gasped and I was yanked forward. I let go of the branch just in time.

Freddie was down even farther. All I could see was his head.

"It's a trap, Alex!"

I desperately searched for something else to use. The flashlight beam was so dim now I could barely see, and tripped over a log.

"Alex! Where are you? Don't leave me!"

"I'm here, Freddie. Hang on."

The log was long enough to cross the mud and rest on the solid ground on either side. I rolled it as close to Freddie's head as possible. "Can you pull your arms out?"

I could hear Freddie grunting and straining.

"Pull! Pull!"

"I am pulling!"

"Pull harder, Freddie!"

"I can't!"

Any second Freddie could be pulled down again. We needed help. I turned toward the palace. "Help! Help! Over here!"

Freddie joined in. We yelled as loudly as we could.

"We're too far away!" cried Freddie. "They'll never get here in time!"

There was no way to reach him from where I was standing. If I rested any part of my body on the log, it might roll right onto Freddie's head.

There had to be another way.

The tree!

Its branches almost reached the mud. I bolted over and started crawling along the trunk. Several branches hung near Freddie — one seemed strong enough to hold my weight. I inched my way along it. A little bit farther. Just a bit more ...

"Keep goin', Alex! You're almost there."

We heard leaves crunching and feet pounding on the ground. "The guards are here!" I shouted. "They'll help you!"

A spear cut through the air and slammed into the tree.

"They're not helping!" screamed Freddie.

An arrow whipped past my head. As I ducked forward, the whole trunk lifted right out of the ground by its roots, throwing me head first into the mud.

Suddenly Freddie and I were plunging down a tunnel. Thick mud poured into our eyes and mouths. We were suffocating.

Just when it felt like our lungs would burst, we splashed into water.

Coughing and spitting, we stood up. "They tried to kill us!"

"I know, but we're okay. Right?"

Freddie's eyes opened wide. "Wrong!"

Guards were running down stone stairs leading from the tree.

"Run!" I shouted.

Freddie and I waded out of the water and took off into a cave.

All around us were icicle-shaped rocks — some hanging from the ceiling, others pushing up from the floor. We ran as fast as we could, jumping over the rocks and moving farther into the cave.

Torches lined the walls. We could see the guards — gaining on us.

As we turned a sharp corner, we saw an opening. Just as we got to it, I remembered what the man in the nursery had said about obstacles stopping anyone from entering the crypt. Something had to be in that chamber. At the last second, I pulled Freddie into a hollow in the cave wall. The guards thudded past us into the chamber.

The footsteps stopped. A muffled voice gasped, "Medusa!" And then everything went quiet.

Freddie looked at me, wide-eyed. "What happened?"

"I don't know."

"Who's Medusa?"

"That name was in one of Dad's books. But I can't remember."

"Think hard," whispered Freddie.

I tried. Then it came to me. "Medusa's a gorgon."

"What's a *gorgon*?"

"Some creature. And Medusa's the main one, I think. She has ... oh yeah, snakes in her hair."

"Ohhh ... no more snakes, please."

"Wait ... wait ... I've got it! If you look at her face, you turn to stone."

Freddie let out a whimper.

That's when it hit us. Everything had gone quiet because the guards had looked at her.

"We gotta get outta here, Alex."

"Brazen shield," I mumbled.

"What?"

"The brazen shield. I read about some guy who used a shield to get past Medusa!"

"What'd he do? Whack her with it?"

"No. He looked at her *reflection* in the shield — not at her — so he was able to fight her. He cut off her head!"

"If those guards turned to stone, she's still got her head."

"You're right."

"Alex, please! Let somebody else get the Eternal Flame." Freddie started back. "We've got half a chance of getting out alive if we go now."

"But we're *so* close!"

"We helped Costas. Isn't that enough?"

"I thought it would be. But —"

"But *what*?"

"It's bigger than just Costas. The *flame* — *that's* why we're here."

"Sorry, Alex. I'm not going in there."

I couldn't blame Freddie. "Okay, you go to the palace."

"The *palace*?"

"If Porteus saw Costas throw the snake out the window, he'd have told Prince Dameon the baby might not be dead. He'll have to make sure! You've got to find the king, tell him everything and show him the way back here."

"Why can't we go together?"

"What if the prince comes here *first*? If he takes the flame and hides it somewhere else, we'll *never* find it."

Freddie nodded but then shook his head. "No! If I go to the palace, they'll kill *me*! You saw what they tried to do at the tree. Those were *real* spears!"

"When you get to the gates, give yourself up. They won't kill you if they know you aren't a threat. Ask to talk to the king and tell him everything."

"He'll never believe me. He'll think I'm part of the plan."

"You have to take that chance, Freddie!"

"*You* take that chance!"

I thought about it for a second. "All right. Then you stay here."

"And do *what*?"

"Wait. If you see the prince and he's got the flame, stop him."

"Are you out of your *mind*?"

"Well, we can't just stand here all night!"

"All right. I'll *go* to the palace. But if I end up locked in the dungeon or stuck on the end of a spear, it'll all be your fault!"

After Freddie had gone, I thought hard. If the prince did come for the flame, he couldn't risk taking it through the palace — he'd *have* to go in and out this way. But I wouldn't stand a chance, especially if he showed up with the secret-society guys. I had to get to the flame first.

Taking a deep breath, I looked at the floor and slowly walked into the chamber. It only took a few seconds before I ran up against something. I reached out and felt it. It was a guard — completely turned to stone.

With my eyes glued to the floor, I spotted a shield with a dragon design on it. But, whatever metal it was made of, it didn't reflect anything.

"And what manner of mortal are you?" asked a sweet voice.

I almost looked up but caught myself just in time. The voice had to belong to Medusa, but I couldn't tell exactly where she was.

"Tell me, little one, where are you from?" She spoke in a soft voice so I wouldn't be afraid.

"No!"

"Why are you angry?"

"I know what you're trying to do!"

"Come, make yourself comfortable. I cannot harm you."

Maybe she couldn't harm me, but *looking* at her could. Dad was right: knowledge is power.

I took a few steps to my left.

"Have you traveled from afar?" Her voice sounded like she was in front of me. I turned another way. "Your clothing is not familiar to me." Now she sounded right beside me.

There had to be some way to figure out exactly where she was.

I saw a flash of light — it only lasted a second. There it was again! What was it? A flame from one of the torches? Yes! Reflected in the glass on my *watch*! Reflected! Just like a mirror!

If I tilted the watch face at a certain angle, I

could see things in it. Part of the room — only a small part — but pretty clear.

"What have you discovered, little one? Some toy?"

I didn't answer, just moved around, looking at the glass. Suddenly I saw the guards — their stone faces frozen in horror, some still in a running position.

As I moved, I saw the reflection of the chamber ceiling and then, when I tilted the watch down a little, a round table. On top of it was a woman's head — just her head.

Her hair was moving — snakes curling and twisting.

"Show it to me." Her voice wasn't soft anymore. "Show me or I shall kill you."

"You can't kill me! I know your secret!"

I walked forward, trying to see behind the table. Yes! An opening in the cave wall!

Keeping as far from Medusa as I could, I made my way to the opening. "You fool!" Her voice was hard and cold. "Go back where you came from!"

"Not without the Eternal Flame," I said through gritted teeth.

"You will *never* reach it. Monstrous things rule in the next chamber."

"You're the monster!"

"Heed my warning. Great effort has been taken to prevent anyone from returning the flame before ..."

"Before what?"

No answer.

"The prince doesn't want the flame returned until he becomes king!" I said. "Then *he'll* return it and everybody'll think he's a hero."

"Ah, you are not such a fool, after all." Medusa laughed a horrible laugh. "Go forward, little one. I await your screams of pain. You'll soon wish you *had* been turned to stone."

I ran behind her, whipped off my jacket and flung it over her head.

Then I walked through the opening.

27

I thought I'd find myself in another chamber, but I was in an open field. Only there wasn't any sky. I was still underground but there were trees and bushes and rocks. Everything was gray — just like the road to Hades. And so silent.

The crypt had to be around here somewhere. I'd come pretty far from the mud-trap entrance, so I was sure I was close. I started walking along a path and headed for a hill in the distance. At the very top, I could see two large doors, deep orange like the autumn leaves on the oak tree in our yard. Remembering made my heart hurt. I wanted to be home. I wanted to see my dad. I wanted things to be normal. It felt like I'd been away forever, and I had no idea if I'd ever get back.

Stop! I had to concentrate.

As I took off toward the hill, something moved.

At first all I saw were three rocks. But then the middle one started to grow. It looked like a body, hunched way over. Then it slowly stood up and looked right at me.

Its eyes were completely black. Like they were hollow.

The face reminded me of a witch in fairy tales, with a long, sharp nose, a pointy chin and warts all over her cheeks. Wisps of straggly gray hair stuck out of her bald head.

The witch raised her arms and started chanting. The sound made the hair on the back of my neck stand up.

As she chanted, a wind came up and a huge cloud began rolling in. As it moved, a long arm reached down from its center and picked up stones and dirt, flinging them into the air.

The whirlwind moved quickly across the field toward me, ripping whole trees out of the ground. The roar got so loud I thought my eardrums would burst. Then the arm reached out for me. I was yanked up in the air and thrown.

My body slammed against something, but it didn't hurt. I felt arms around me, holding me. Then I was quickly lowered to the ground.

When the dust cleared, I saw soldiers standing in a circle around the witch. They wore helmets and breastplates and their bows were ready to shoot. Freddie was standing behind them with a man dressed in a long blue cloak trimmed in gold.

Freddie smiled and said, "He believed me!"

Not knowing quite what to do, I bowed.

King Talasius smiled. His dark eyes looked gentle. "It is I who should bow to you ... and your friend. You have both shown great courage."

Freddie and I never thought we'd hear a king say that.

"Do those doors lead to the crypt?" I asked, pointing up the hill.

He nodded. "They do."

"The Eternal Flame is burning at your father's sarcophagus."

"I would never have believed my brother to be so devious," said the king. "I have underestimated him greatly."

He turned to his soldiers and was just about to say something when the witch made a motion with her hands and then blew into the air. The soldiers, their bows still drawn, suddenly turned and shot each other!

Horrified, the king staggered back. Freddie and I grabbed him and pushed him behind a rock. We stayed low and watched as all the soldiers fell, writhing and moaning in pain.

"What *happened*?" cried Freddie.

The witch sank to her knees. "I call upon the spirits of death. Keres be set upon you!"

The king's eyes opened wide. "Keres!"

Before I could ask what they were, the earth groaned and, with a loud shriek, dark shapes rose out of the ground, their eyes a shimmering white against their black faces. With a quick movement, they sprang at the bodies of the dying soldiers.

Some Keres hovered over the bodies that tried to fight back. Then they let out ferocious screeches and pounced on them.

King Talasius quickly led us to a grove of burned trees. Beyond it was a stone wall. We ran over, climbed it, then crouched on the other side. Suddenly, one of the Keres vaulted over the wall, landing right in front of us.

Freddie and I screamed. The Kere sniffed at us.

"Wh— what's it doing?" Freddie's voice was trembling.

"It will only attack the injured," said the king. "She must smell blood first."

Without taking his eyes off the Kere, he motioned for us to move toward the hill. When we got there, it turned out to be a huge rock with steps carved into it. Freddie and I quickly climbed the stairs.

The doors had no handles.

"How are we gonna get in?" cried Freddie.

A flaming torch stood on either side. "Maybe they turn or something and that makes the doors open," I suggested.

We each took a torch — turning and twisting and lifting the iron rings they rested in. Nothing.

"We're never gonna get in!" Freddie pounded his fist on the stone.

Just then the doors parted and Prince Dameon burst through. Freddie and I flattened ourselves against the wall so he wouldn't see us. The prince held a large torch. The Eternal Flame!

As he looked out over the field he smiled, then quickly went down the steps. At the bottom he found himself face to face with the king.

He stopped cold.

The brothers looked at each other for a long time before King Talasius spoke. His voice sounded sad. "Why have you done this?"

"Why?" The prince's eyes narrowed. "I will tell you *why*, dear brother ... I refuse to live in your illustrious shadow." His voice sounded full of hatred.

"You have not made your mark in the eyes of our nation, that is true," said the king. "But that is because you have wasted your talents and chosen to live a life without meaning, without honor."

"When glory and adulation are poured upon you, it is not difficult to lead an honorable life. But I … I have received *nothing*!"

The king frowned. "All that you have desired has been given to you."

"Not … *power*."

"When what you have done is discovered, *none* will follow you."

Prince Dameon looked toward the field of dead soldiers. "Only you have this knowledge."

"And your secret society?" asked the king.

"Poisoned. None is left to tell."

Hearing that, the king looked even sadder.

"The throne *will* be mine." With one quick motion, the prince drew his sword. The king stepped back.

"And soon *no one* will know."

He raised his sword.

"We'll know!"

As Prince Dameon spun around, his eyes wide with surprise, I aimed my torch like a spear and threw as hard as I could. It flew straight at the prince. When his arm shot up to protect his face, the sharp edge of his sword cut his forehead.

The Eternal Flame fell to the ground.

With a loud cry, the prince turned to the

king. Just as his arm went to plunge the sword, the Keres pounced on him, dragging him away. His screams echoed across the field.

Freddie and I slowly went down the stairs and picked up the still-burning flame. The king's eyes were filled with tears.

28

The Sacred Hearth sprang to life as flames burned strong and beautiful. Under the bright sun, the village had gathered. The king walked beside the queen as she carried their baby. Both had radiant smiles.

Choirs sang and girls threw flowers as they danced along the path. Then came the sound of pipes and flutes. Everyone looked so happy.

The king and queen walked three times around the hearth. Then King Talasius spoke. "Out of compassion for mankind, Prometheus brought down fire from the sun and placed it here upon the Sacred Hearth of Hestia. Families large and small, from far and wide, gather here to name their beloved children. Throughout our long history, many souls have lived and passed, but this blessed fire has remained forever burning.

"The Eternal Flame shall welcome every soul that comes upon this earth. Animals must look down, but man, made of divine substance, can turn his eyes to the heavens." The king took the baby and held him high. Then, looking up at the clear blue sky, he said, "On this glorious day, I, King Talasius, give to my firstborn son the name … Alexander."

A shiver went through my body. A prince had been named after me.

After a grand feast, Freddie and I were taken to the Sacred River. Looking out at the most spectacular sunset, we walked into the water. When it reached our shoulders, we turned and looked back. Standing on the shore, in shimmering light, stood Tiresias and Costas, smiling.

As Freddie and I slid under the water, we felt our bodies moving at a terrific speed. Then we saw a golden light. It got bigger and brighter, and all around us sounded sweet music. Something opened inside me, and I felt happier and safer than I'd felt in my whole life.

With a sudden rush, a powerful force pushed us out of the water. It shot us through the night sky, in my bedroom door, across the room and slammed us on the bed. Freddie and I lay there, stunned.

My right hand, jammed under the pillow, felt something round and cool. I pulled it out. Mr. Lucas's gold coin!

"Wh— where'd you go?" a frightened voice asked.

Freddie and I looked over the edge of the bed. There was Slug, cowering in the corner, shaking like a leaf.

"He wants to know where we went."

Freddie rested his chin on his hands. "Should we tell him?"

"Okay."

"What if he tells somebody?"

I slowly shook my head. "They'll *never* believe him."

29

On opening night, people lined up around the block to get into Oddities. Mr. Lucas and some of the old folks from the nursing home came. He was fine — it was *not* taking his medications that had made him go nutty. They found a sock full of pills in his drawer. When I offered him his gold coin back, he said he was more than happy to let the corpse keep it. Said it made him feel a part of something big.

Having the corpse on exhibit *was* big. Everybody in town came to see it. Some people swore it was the same corpse they'd seen run through their yards on Halloween night. One lady even fainted when she saw it. Reporters were taking notes like crazy, and there were cameras everywhere. Freddie gave interviews. Folks said he knew so much about ancient Greece, you'd think he'd been there.

Slug showed up at Oddities with his parents. Something happened to him that night in my bedroom. Whatever it was changed him. Maybe, for the first time, he knew what it meant to be scared. I don't know. But he never asked for money again. Not from me, or anybody else.

And Rosalie? Well, she tried for days to wheedle out of me where I'd been when I called. But my secret made me mysterious. The less I said, the more interested she got. Go figure. She even agreed to be my date on opening night.

With each exhibit we saw, she moved closer and closer. By the time we'd gone through the Goraporium and the Corn Maze, we were practically attached.

Then, as we headed for the corpse, Rosalie's hand found mine … and she held on tight.

Also by L.M. Falcone
The Mysterious Mummer

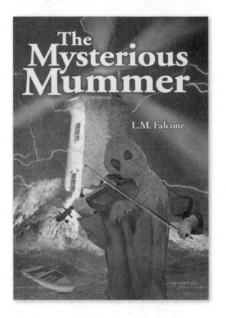

"Did you hear what I said?!" I was shouting now. "Something really strange is going on here!"

Thirteen-year-old Joey McDermet isn't exactly feeling festive this holiday season. He's stuck with his aunt in "small town" Newfoundland for the holidays, which is bad enough, but now her bizarre behavior is really starting to make him nervous. The house is a mess, there's an altar in the bedroom and Aunt Corinne spends an awful lot of time at the edge of the cliff overlooking the ocean where her husband drowned.

And that's just the beginning of what becomes a very creepy Christmas. Mysterious goings-on at the local lighthouse, eerie townsfolk popping in and out of the fog and a couple of downright peculiar Yuletide traditions lure Jocy deeper and deeper into a world where history and mystery are about to collide!

"A lively pace, intriguing details of life (and death) in a small coastal town, an engaging protagonist, and some genuinely creepy plot twists inform this gothic thriller."

— *School Library Journal*